Mormon Misfits

LGBTQ Mormons may not be a good fit for the LDS world, but there's plenty of room for them elsewhere.

A budding feminist tries to make a political statement by giving birth to her "illegitimate" son in church just before Mother's Day. A gay man works with unhoused people in Seattle while taking care of a terminally ill partner at home. A lesbian couple fight internalized homophobia that has them questioning if their desperate financial situation is a punishment from God. A man trains himself to stop praying. A gay man falls in love in Morocco. Another man learns his boyfriend was at a nightclub when a mass shooter attacked.

Few of us are a perfect fit for the culture we're born into, yet even as religious intolerance makes a desperate comeback attempt, there are good, like-minded folks everywhere. And love always wins in the end.

Praise for Johnny Townsend

In *Zombies for Jesus*, "Townsend isn't writing satire, but deeply emotional and revealing portraits of people who are, with a few exceptions, quite lovable."

Kel Munger, *Sacramento News and Review*

In *Sex among the Saints,* "Townsend writes with a deadpan wit and a supple, realistic prose that's full of psychological empathy….he takes his protagonists' moral struggles seriously and invests them with real emotional resonance."

Kirkus Reviews

Inferno in the French Quarter: The UpStairs Lounge Fire is "a gripping account of all the horrors that transpired that night, as well as a respectful remembrance of the victims."

Terry Firma, Patheos

"Johnny Townsend's 'Partying with St. Roch' [in the anthology *Latter-Gay Saints*] tells a beautiful, haunting tale."

Kent Brintnall, Out in Print: Queer Book Reviews

Selling the City of Enoch is "sharply intelligent…pleasingly complex…The stories are full of…doubters, but there's no vindictiveness in these pages; the characters continuously poke holes in Mormonism's more extravagant absurdities, but they take very little pleasure in doing so….Many of Townsend's stories…have a provocative edge to them, but this [book] displays a great deal of insight as well…a playful, biting and surprisingly warm collection."

Kirkus Reviews

Gayrabian Nights is "an allegorical tour de force…a hard-core emotional punch."

Gay. Guy. Reading and Friends

The Washing of Brains has "A lovely writing style, and each story [is] full of unique, engaging characters….immensely entertaining."

Rainbow Awards

In *Dead Mankind Walking*, "Townsend writes in an energetic prose that balances crankiness and humor….A rambunctious volume of short, well-crafted essays…"

Kirkus Reviews

Mormon Misfits

Johnny Townsend

Print ISBN: 979-8-9883389-6-3
Ebook ISBN: 979-8-9883389-7-0

[Selected stories from *The Washing of Brains*, *The Last Days Linger*, and *The Moat around Zion*.]

This book is a work of fiction. Names, characters, events, and dialogue are the product of the author's imagination or are used fictitiously. Any resemblance to actual persons, living or dead, is entirely coincidental.

Printed on acid-free paper.

2023

First Edition

Cover design by BetiBup33 Studio Design

Contents

The Girl from Treponema

The young woman at the window grimaced in my direction, giving her best approximation of a smile, her teeth showing a long history of meth. She didn't need to tell me her name. Some customers one remembered instantly. I pulled Cathy up on the computer and saw that she had three pieces of mail waiting, two regular and one DSHS.

We separated the mail for more than 3000 clients according to type: 1st class, DSHS checks, special, oversize, Affordable Care, EBT cards, and so forth. Most of the people who came to Mailing Address were homeless, or addicts, or mentally ill, sometimes all three.

I had Cathy sign for her check, handed her the mail, and wished her a good day. Since I knew she liked macaroni and cheese, I also handed her a coupon before she walked away. I tried to clip a few coupons every week for the items I knew various customers liked, though I only had time to hand them out if the line wasn't too long.

I quickly flipped through my small stack to make sure I still had the one for kitchenware. Sharonda was due to stop by sometime over the next few days. She had a phobia about washing dishes. Rather than rinse her pots and pans, she'd set them out in her back yard so the food wouldn't stink up her apartment as it rotted. When all the pots from her kitchen were eventually outside, she'd either break down and wash or, more often, go out and buy new ones.

Last week, she'd come in crying, saying that when she went to go set out her latest pan, she discovered someone had stolen all the others sitting in the yard. I'd started looking for coupons as soon as I returned home. She could always go to Goodwill, of course, but she wouldn't be caught dead eating from pots someone else had cooked in.

A Hispanic man came up to the window next, so I used the Spanish I'd learned on my mission to Honduras decades ago and that I practiced with my husband now. The man withdrew $60 from his account and shoved it into his pocket.

The morning dragged on, one client after another after another appearing at the window. I opened an account for a guy who wanted to deposit $20 "for emergencies," and I handed out a daily allowance for one of our payees who wasn't able to budget his own money.

"Time for your lunch break, Buddy," said Chryssie, another one of the tellers, coming to relieve me. This week, Chryssie had blond hair with magenta trim, making her look younger than her forty years. She and I took turns throughout the day, working the window, sorting and labeling mail, and then going back to the window. There were three tellers, three case managers, our actual manager, and a couple of volunteers on any given day.

"Thanks. I'll be back in half an hour." I grabbed my jacket and headed out the building. Most of the others ate in the mail room, and I usually did, too, but lately, I'd felt the need to get away for a few minutes each day. I'd been working here over ten years, ever since moving to Seattle after Hurricane Katrina destroyed my apartment and thousands of other homes in New Orleans.

One my coworkers there had been unable to face starting over at forty-six and killed herself. I'd been only forty-five at the time and had used half of my savings to buy a ticket to Seattle, once the computers in Hammond were up and running again.

The sun was shining brightly in Seattle today, and the temperature had warmed to over fifty degrees. I looked out over the Sound, the snow-capped Olympics on the far side. Working in Pioneer Square, right on the water, was always a little nerve-wracking. These were the oldest buildings in town, all vulnerably brick, built above "underground Seattle."

The early inhabitants had suffered so many problems with the water, spouting toilets for one, that they'd eventually built a street one floor up over the original city. People could still visit the former ground level buildings for a fee, interesting enough, but I was never able to get the idea out of my mind that in any sizeable earthquake, we'd all be the first to go. If we weren't killed by the quake itself, there was always the tsunami we were unlikely to escape.

Things like devastating hurricanes had a way of warping how one viewed the world.

I knew Antonio was going to die.

I turned the corner and walked up to 1st Avenue, passing a chunky black guy masturbating in an alleyway. A few feet farther on, a white guy in a wheelchair, with two prosthetic legs, was urinating against the side of a building. He seemed unperturbed that his stream was hitting his feet as well.

I ducked into a Thai restaurant and ordered. There was no lack of eateries in the neighborhood. One served passable New Orleans cuisine, but I could never eat there without thinking of

Don, who'd died of pancreatic cancer just before the hurricane hit. Even after all the time we'd been together, he hadn't left a will, so his brother inherited the house and the car, and I moved into a tiny apartment in St. Roch.

My friends had warned me against the neighborhood, about 97% black, but ethnicity had not turned out to be the problem. I'd just bought a stackable washer and dryer, the most expensive available because it was also the smallest, when I had to evacuate by bus, taking just one suitcase. I'd never seen my apartment again.

I sat near the plate glass window facing 1st Avenue, watching people walk by. At least half of them were tourists, oblivious to the other half who were destitute. This was the only neighborhood I could afford when I'd moved here in 2005. Then I met Antonio and we bought a house together in Hillman City, the first house for either of us in our own names.

He was a laborer, mostly cement work, still hunky at fifty, but breathing had become more and more difficult over the last year, and finally I was able to convince him to see a doctor.

The career I'd wanted to have. Back in the mid-90s, I'd dated a guy with full-blown AIDS and become frustrated with both the care and the information available to patients. "Do you think both sides of your brain work?" Stevens asked while we were shopping one evening for a new pillbox. He still used make-up then to hide the black Kaposi's marks.

"What do you mean?" I'd asked. I tried to remember what the right side of the brain was responsible for.

"Why don't you go to medical school so you can be sure I get the treatment I need?"

I'd already earned three English degrees by this point and was an adjunct at two different schools, but I enrolled in remedial math and started over again.

Stevens was dead by my third semester. But I kept at it. Physics, anatomy, histology, statistics. I remembered struggling with chemistry, irritated when the solution in the back of the book was different from my answer on a homework assignment. I went over the problem again and again, and I kept coming up with the same wrong answer.

So I stopped by the professor's office to ask about it, and he said dismissively, "You're right, obviously. The book's wrong," and ushered me out the door in a manner indicating he thought I was being a show-off. It had never occurred to me I might actually be good at this stuff.

A couple of semesters later, it had been excruciating in Genetics class to have to tell the professor after every single exam that he'd graded my answers incorrectly. He always said, "Oh, I see. You're absolutely right. Sorry about that," and adjusted my grade. Was that really supposed to be my job?

Only a few minutes left for lunch. I pulled out my cell and called Antonio. "How's my honey feeling today?" I asked. He'd lost at least forty pounds in the past six months.

"Not so good, Buddy. I tried to pull some dandelions in the yard and got winded in five minutes."

"Don't worry about it," I said. "I'll take care of it."

"But you're doing everything," Antonio protested. "I'm not dead yet."

I stared out the window. A man with a huge herpes lesion on his face walked by. "I wish…" I said. "I wish…"

"There's no wishing," Antonio said sternly. "And there's no praying."

I'd hung onto a belief in God decades after being excommunicated from the Mormon Church, but these last few years, I'd joined Antonio in becoming an atheist. Still, enough residual Mormonism lingered to make me wish he'd never taken up smoking when he was a teen. "Want anything special for dinner tonight?" I asked.

"I'll fix burritos," he replied. "You like my burritos."

So did he. I'd suggested months ago that we eat his favorite foods every day. That meant tacos five to six days a week, and burritos when he was feeling depressed. "See you in a few hours."

"Love you, Buddy."

I walked back to Mailing Address, put in the code to the office door, and reopened my window. "Arthur was here," Chryssie said. "He was asking for you."

Arthur was one of our regulars who came almost every day. He only received at best three pieces of mail a month. He didn't come for that, of course. He came because we were his only social outlet.

I found some mail for the next customer, but one piece was missing. With over twenty boxes of mail spread out all over the office, there was no telling where it was, or if we'd already given it to the customer and simply forgotten to scan it. Two people withdrew money, one deposited money, three asked if they had any mail but didn't, and four more people picked up checks.

During a lull, I logged in fifteen new EBT cards we received today.

"Need you back at the window," said Tyresia, just out of college and working here almost six weeks now. She still acted like a student, studying at work just for fun when things were slow. I couldn't remember what it was like to be that young.

I pulled up the metal grid over the adjoining station and asked an Asian man if I could help him. He thrust his ID at me without saying a word. Lots of the customers never talked to us. Which was often better than if they did.

The next person asked where he could take a dump, and I directed him to our Hygiene Center downstairs, where customers could use the bathroom or bring their laundry. The staff in that department handled all the laundry, at no charge, of course. They just had to wear thick gloves when emptying the customers' pockets, because of the needles.

Telling people where to go to the bathroom. It was a far cry from curing HIV infections. Or treating cancer.

Or prolonging life in a way that was more than just existence.

I thought back to my Cell Physiology class, where the professor had been so consumed with a textbook he was writing that he completely abandoned students in the lab. We tried to figure everything out on our own, but every single one of us received low marks for that portion of the grade. I had the highest GPA in the class by the end of the semester, and even I ended up with a B.

I wondered if I should buy some ice cream for Antonio on the way home. I never had any myself, needing to keep in shape.

But Grocery Outlet had a sale on Häagen-Dazs for 99 cents a pint. Tres Leches, Antonio's favorite.

Of course, his taste buds weren't working well these days because of the medication.

I'd wanted to save the world.

I remembered my Biochemistry class, the single hardest class in over twelve years of college courses, far harder than Organic Chemistry, which had been kind of fun. But Biochem—sheesh. I'd made out over five hundred note cards while hunched in my library cubicle, drawing each of the molecules I needed to understand. I learned dozens of complicated pathways and knew every step, able to draw every molecule from start to finish.

I interviewed five years in a row for medical school. In the end, the dean told me I just didn't have the right personality to be a physician. It was a terrible blow, and the insecurity from all those years as a Mormon, constantly being told I never measured up, came flooding back. But then I met Don, an ex-JW, and I worked hard to leave the last vestiges of Mormonism behind me forever.

Mail was sorted for the day, so all three teller windows were now open. I asked Susie about her Chihuahua with cataracts while I withdrew money for her, asked José about his aunt who'd been having seizures, and asked Phuc about his new job at a warehouse in Sodo.

But mostly, I just smiled and handled the transactions as quickly as I could to keep the line down. With three of us at the window, things moved along smoothly.

"What did you think of that windstorm the other day?" Chryssie asked during a slow spell. A man had been killed in Seward Park when a tree landed on his car.

I thought of an old boyfriend in Lakeview who'd drowned in his attic.

"Freaky," said Tyresia. She began talking about how the storm had knocked over all her daffodils.

"You okay, Buddy?" Chryssie asked. Tyresia turned to stare at me.

"I think I might leave early, if that's okay with you guys."

"Sure, sure, we'll see you tomorrow. Feel better."

I clocked off the computer and picked up my jacket before heading back out the door. An obese man in a motorized wheelchair was staring at rust-colored water bubbling out of a manhole on the street. I turned the corner and saw three gobs of spit in a row on the sidewalk. I trudged up to the gem and fossil shop on 1st, looking through the window at a three-foot high geode, the purple amethyst crystals forming a breathtaking cave.

A piece of natural artwork I could never afford as a nobody making minimum wage. I looked about me, at the intricate brick, stone, and cement work around the windows, doors, and along the roof lines of most of the buildings in the area. For a dilapidated neighborhood, it was still quite beautiful here. Things could be worse.

I thought about the blood Antonio sometimes coughed up.

A long-haired Native American man walked past with a short Latino man, sharing a cigarette. They were followed by a well-tailored white man who trotted up the steps to a law firm. A professional making a difference in the world. Then a middle-aged woman probably only a couple of years younger than I was tapped me on the shoulder. Pus was oozing from a sore on her face.

I thought of my Microbiology class, where we had to bring samples of our own *E. coli* to culture in Petri dishes. I'd sung "The Girl from Treponema" to my lab partner during one class. She'd laughed, wagging her finger and saying, "Better watch out for her!"

I'd also volunteered to correct the lab manual the professor had written. Lots of grammar errors on every page. But I realized now that my offer had probably been obnoxious.

"Come on," I said to the woman, putting my hand on her arm. She was someone I'd never seen before. "Let's get you signed up for some help." I walked back with her to Mailing Address and stood with her in line until Chryssie's window was free. She was still the best at registration. And she could set the woman up with a case manager after she finished.

I walked five blocks to the bus stop near the old train station and headed for Grocery Outlet, where I picked up that pint of ice cream I needed to make sure Antonio knew how much I loved him.

The Laban Justification

I was two weeks away from finishing my mission to Moscow when President Carruthers ordered me to the mission home for an emergency interview. "Elder Miller," I told my companion, "I think the jig is up." I looked down into his shocked face. He was only 5'6", three full inches shorter than I was, but he had a strength which always made him seem taller, even now when we might be facing excommunication.

"*Blin!*" Elder Miller said after I hung up the phone. "Elder Olson, if you go down, I'm going down with you." He put his hand on my arm.

Going down was part of the problem.

In some ways, my call to Russia had been a godsend. All the missionaries here used the title of Elder or Sister, so I never had to tell anyone my first name. It had been difficult growing up in Sandy, Utah with the name Laban. While it was no longer terribly common for Latter-day Saints to give their kids names from the Book of Mormon, when they did, it was usually Ammon or Samuel or Nephi or the name of some other hero.

Laban, of course, was the bad guy murdered by Nephi at the command of God, for refusing to hand over the family history to Lehi. "It is better that one man should perish than that a nation should dwindle and perish in unbelief." So off came his head.

My parents, clandestine liberals, in an attempt to make Nephi's murder more humane, had named me after a villain. "We need to restore life to the man who died to give us the Book of Mormon," my mom told me when I complained the first time kids at church teased me.

"Because of you," my dad repeated when I complained the twentieth time, "Laban lives on."

It wasn't much consolation. But out here in the mission field, I could be a normal person for the first time in my life. Elder Olson.

And then Elder Miller had been assigned to me just as I was nearing the end of my mission. After three days with him, I had to face the fact I was never going to be normal, whatever my name. I was still gay despite two years of dedicated service to the Lord, and I knew almost instantly I wanted to marry Elder Miller.

He still had a year left, but after we made love for over an hour on our two-month anniversary, I told him I would faithfully wait for him back home until his return. He smiled and said, "And I promise I won't have sex with any other missionaries until we're both together in Salt Lake again."

"Then you'll start having sex with the missionaries on Temple Square?" I teased.

He tweaked my nipple, and I almost cried out. Given that the district leader and his companion were on the other side of a very thin wall, that might have proved awkward. But since President Carruthers was demanding to see me now, it looked like we'd been overheard at some point, after all. We'd had three and a half great months together, though, and even the shame of being sent home dishonorably couldn't change that.

Or our commitment to marry.

I put my arm around his shoulders. They were heavily muscled, as was most of Miller's body. He was no Aleksey Lesukov, though I felt safe with him on the street, knowing that potential *khuligany* would be intimidated. I suspected he was overcompensating for his height by working out during Quiet Hour every morning instead of studying. My own body wasn't as firm, but my companion never made me feel less attractive because of it.

"I hope I haven't ruined your life," Elder Miller said softly. "Do you think the president knows?"

"Teancum," I whispered, "you're the best thing that ever happened to me. No matter what." A love song from Alla Pugacheva drifted through the wall from a neighbor's apartment, and I smiled.

"He's not asking *me* to see him. It can't be about our relationship."

I leaned over and kissed him. "For couples, everything is about our relationship."

It had been miraculous to discover our attraction, then our love, and ultimately, that we'd both been cursed with horrific first names. Despite the years of teasing Elder Miller had already suffered, it was impossible not to ask for "tea and cum" when we made love. As it turned out, he gave me "cum and tea" instead, a full load of semen in my rectum, followed by a stream of urine.

I'd been quite startled the first time, but now the activity was just a normal part of our nightly routine. Afterward, my companion would give me "head." Of course, the way he put it was, "I'll give you back your head." A stupid pun that should have made me groan, but I smiled every time he said it.

"When does the president want to see you?" Elder Miller asked.

"Right away," I said. Then I paused.

"What is it?"

"He asked me to come by myself, leave you with the other two elders. He's not even asking the district leader to come with me."

"How strange," Elder Miller mused. "Missionaries never go anywhere alone."

My companion was right. If this was about Miller and me, we'd both have been summoned. Something else was up. Even so, asking me to come alone was odd. "I guess I'd better get moving." I shrugged. "It'll take an hour to get to the mission home from here."

It was early summer, already quite hot, with a thick haze from a nearby forest fire hanging over the city. I decided not to wear my suit jacket, despite the formality of meeting with President Carruthers. If it was bad news, a coat wouldn't make a difference in any event. Serving a mission here had been eye-opening, so few baptisms, and so many members going inactive.

My parents were always sending me updates on General Authorities who grew ever more ancient and feeble but who were still forced to fly to different states almost weekly in an attempt to stop the leakage. There was a "Boise Rescue" and a "Denver Rescue" and a "San Jose Rescue." Buddies from my ward serving missions in Spain and Bulgaria and Japan were all telling me members were leaving. The zone leaders let slip just a couple of weeks ago that the Church had dissolved the one existing stake in Armenia.

It was difficult not to worry that the Church itself was dying. Elder Miller and I would be leaving Mormonism behind as soon as we finished our missions, since no one in the Church would want us once they knew our secret. But we were still doing our best to build the Kingdom while we could.

It wasn't about getting bonus points with God, though. It was kind of like when my grandpa planted an oak tree the day my sister married and moved into her first home, even though he knew he'd never benefit from the tree himself.

I stepped off the metro below Muravskaya and climbed up to the street. A charcoal-colored Lada drove by, and I paused to admire it. I didn't want to be sent home. In fact, I didn't want to go back to Utah at all. No one could *make* me leave Russia. I could try to get a job here teaching English or something and keep attending Elder Miller's ward.

Of course, it was quite likely he'd be transferred another two or three more times before the end of his mission. I could hardly become a nomadic wanderer teaching English on street corners. Perhaps it would be best to go back to Salt Lake, enroll at the U, and find an apartment we could share when he finally joined me.

For the first time, I understood what it must be like for parents to be away from their kids for two years.

I slowly walked the last ten minutes to the mission home, taking in the cars and passersby and the sound of muffled Russian conversations. Mission headquarters was on the third floor of a rather boring building. I began trembling as I climbed the stairs. Sister Carruthers opened the door with a smile and ushered me in, so motherly I couldn't help but start to feel safe again. She looked as if she hadn't gained a single pound despite bearing five children, the youngest two still teenagers living here in the mission home with them. "Go on into his office, dear," she said sweetly in English. "He's expecting you."

I walked carefully down the hall, passing one of the AP's. Elder Grenier was from Marseille and the first decent Assistant to the President we'd had during the last two years. So many elders in the mission hierarchy let their power go to their heads. Our last zone leader took to making prophecies about the rest of us during zone conference.

Always way off the mark, but then he would just blame us for our lack of faith when they didn't come true. Elder Grenier looked at me curiously now but still smiled in his usual friendly way. I knocked on the president's door and heard a deep voice call back gruffly. "Come in, Elder Olson."

How did he know it was me and not one of the office staff, I wondered? Maybe he really did have the power of discernment. I realized with a sinking feeling this was probably not going to turn out well, whatever he knew or didn't know at this point. I pushed the door open and went in.

President Carruthers, a trim man in his upper fifties, sat behind his desk, his hands clasped, looking very serious. He'd served in the Air Force for years and was all about order. Even when missionaries made the smallest infractions, he called us out on them in our quarterly interviews. We had to read our mission rulebook at least once a week and mark it on our stat sheet.

I could only imagine what the man would say if he learned what Miller and I were up to. One of the rules was to love our companions, but I expected the president wouldn't appreciate our interpretation of the law.

In front of the president's desk sat another gentleman in an expensive suit, a Russian, maybe in his forties, a bit stocky, probably a local member. The president wasn't wearing his jacket, but the Russian wore one, and something told me this wasn't a good sign. Did he have some grievance with me? I didn't even recognize him. The president stood, and we shook hands across his desk. He motioned to the other man, and the two of us shook hands as well.

"*Zdravstvujtye*," I said. "I'm Elder Olson."

"You don't need to know this gentleman's name," the president interjected, still in Russian. "Please sit."

All three of us took our seats, while I looked from the Russian to the president and back to the Russian again. "*Zdarova*?" I asked.

"Elder Olson," President Carruthers began, "the Lord has a special mission for you."

Boy, he wasn't wasting any time. But at least he wasn't talking about sex. Perhaps this was an emergency transfer. Sometimes other elders were constantly at each other's throats and had to be separated. Then a "gentle" elder had to go in. It had happened to me twice before, but this time I would have to get out of it. "I've only got two weeks left," I reminded him.

"We need you to make a deal with some guys in the Russian mafia."

"Excuse me?" I turned to look at the Russian man, whose face remained blank. I clearly hadn't heard right. So many words in Russian were difficult to make out, even after all this time. I turned back to the president.

"It's going to be very dangerous, Elder. That's why we want a missionary to do it. If you're killed while on your mission, you automatically qualify for the Celestial Kingdom."

That I understood. I frowned and looked more deeply into the president's eyes. Unlike the other elders, this man did receive inspiration for all the missionaries serving under him. Knowing that Outer Darkness probably awaited me as a fallen gay Mormon, I found the idea intriguing. Still, there was no point in going to the Celestial Kingdom if Elder Miller wasn't there.

Sometimes missionaries had special assignments like finding a building where we could open a new branch or, more often, find a smaller one when we had to downsize. Sometimes, we were asked to translate Church literature, or interpret when "greenies" had to see a doctor or experienced a problem with their visas. But nothing like this.

I couldn't help but suspect that another reason the president wanted a missionary for this assignment was that if I were caught by authorities, whatever crime I was committing could more easily be passed off as the act of a stupid young American. I continued frowning.

"This gentleman will tell you where to go and who to meet," President Carruthers said. "Then you'll probably be driven somewhere with a hood over your head to meet some other people, who will then take you to meet someone else. God only knows what'll happen next or where you'll end up." He sighed. "But what we hope is that you'll eventually be brought to the right men and be able to negotiate the purchase of three nuclear devices. You know, some of the ones that 'disappeared' when the Soviet Union collapsed."

I closed my eyes tightly and shook my head to clear it. I was here to bring souls to God, not participate in international intrigue. Why wasn't this something the CIA was doing instead of me? I'd heard that returned missionaries were often recruited by intelligence services, but I wasn't an RM yet.

And surely an American would be sitting next to me instead of a Russian if I were being recruited right now. I had a reasonable talent with the language and could probably polish it up a bit more if I were allowed to study it instead of my discussions, but this assignment would clearly involve the use of many words I wouldn't know. Why didn't this Russian guy do the negotiating himself?

Then suddenly I felt my heart responding in recognition to the truth the way it did the first time I'd tested Moroni's promise. I was being asked because my life was less valuable. Perhaps the president did know I was gay.

"How will I get the bombs to Moscow?" I asked. "Or wherever it is you want them? And why exactly *do* you want them?" Mormons had killed people before, of course, back at Mountain Meadows, and we'd had the Mormon Battalion before that, but flat-out bombing people seemed extreme. Then again, the Book of Mormon showed the Nephites slaughtering hundreds of thousands, even millions, in the name of God.

And wasn't there a story in the Old Testament where God commanded the Jews to circumcise all the men among a group they were pretending to assimilate, and then kill them all while they were too sore to fight back? One never really knew what Heavenly Father was going to demand.

The two men exchanged glances. "Normally, this would be on a need-to-know basis," the president said slowly. "And the Russians don't want me to tell you any more than I already have. But since you're risking your life, I suppose you deserve the truth. We're always taught to be honest in our dealings with our fellow men."

I frowned again, not sure I was buying any of this. From the movies I'd seen, the people most at risk were always kept in the dark. Even the early Saints were lied to about Joseph Smith's polygamy. *Chert*, even members today were lied to until a couple of years ago.

My parents had told me about Joseph's long-denied wives years before I heard the Church admit anything. I wondered what would happen if I said no to the president. Or what might happen if I said no after I heard everything he had to say.

I felt a chill. I wanted to hold Elder Miller.

"It's global warming," President Carruthers said simply. "Turns out it's real."

"Yeah?" I tried not to sound surly but I couldn't fully control my tone. My parents had believed the science for years, but I'd never met many other Mormons who felt the same. Even those who did always just shrugged and said, "Heavenly Father will take care of everything." So what was I supposed to do now? Destroy oil refineries in Saudi Arabia? None of this was making any sense.

"Elder Olson, you know how strongly we Saints take the call to be stewards of the Earth." He chuckled, but there was no mirth in the sound. "The Prophet in Salt Lake has spoken directly to me about what must be done."

I tried not to show my surprise. The Prophet had barely spoken for five minutes at each of the last two General Conferences. It was difficult to tell if he was even able to follow the proceedings. But then there was no real reason Heavenly Father couldn't step in and restore his health when it was needed.

"He said he fell asleep watching *Nova*, and when he woke up, he knew what had to be done," President Carruthers explained. "He says we must act immediately if we hope to avoid total disaster for the entire planet."

I thought hard for a second but couldn't connect the dots. The Book of Mormon had one brief passage about the need for the Nephites to reforest the land after they'd foolishly used up all the natural resources, but it was only my parents who ever talked to me about issues like that. I never heard such things mentioned in Sunday School.

"So who are we going to blow up?" It was either the policies of the American government or those of Chinese leaders which were causing the most carbon pollution, if I remembered news stories I'd heard before my mission. Of course, we were never allowed to read newspapers or watch TV out here, and the situation might have changed in the past two years. Was I going to help deliver nukes to Washington, DC and Beijing and Lord only knew what other godforsaken city?

Der'mo. Surely, I wasn't seriously considering going along with any of this. I just wanted to go tracting with Elder Miller.

Split a vatrushka with him while on break and lick the kvark off his lips.

I'd been shocked the first time Elder Miller sucked me off and then kissed me before swallowing. That had been even better than kvark. He swore he'd been a virgin before we met, but he seemed so confident, so experienced, and all I could think of sometimes was how much more we'd know after ten years together, after—

The Russian man leaned toward me and whispered, "Yellowstone." I could barely understand his pronunciation.

"Elder Olson," the president went on, "you may not know this, but the Earth is warming at an incredible rate."

"Yes, I did know," I replied. "Didn't you?" I wondered why David O. McKay hadn't said something about it in the 1950's when it might have made a difference. For that matter, why hadn't my parents done anything themselves? Why hadn't I when they told me?

"All nations must work together to slow it down immediately and ultimately reverse it."

I looked at the Russian, who must either be a government agent or tied up somehow with the Mafia. Was this Heavenly Father's way of forcing everyone to make peace with one another? I'd always been taught that coercing people to do the right thing was Satan's plan.

"Sacrifices have to be made."

I'd never heard any of this urgency in General Conference.

I bit my lip. Maybe that was because I'd been lazy as a teenager and never watched every session. Even for the devout, those conferences were awfully tedious. But I would've heard something from the beehive if anything momentous had ever been stated. My folks often pointed out that none of the prophets had said much of anything consequential in over a hundred and fifty years.

The dots still weren't connecting.

"Heavenly Father knows our actions will help prepare the world for the Second Coming. When Gospodin Ivano—" The man held up a hand and President Carruthers stopped. "When the Prophet approached me with a plan, I located this man and asked for his help."

"I don't understand." I was sweating, and it wasn't only because of the increasingly stuffy atmosphere in the room.

President Carruthers rubbed his hands together as if cold. "We have to set off three nuclear weapons in Yellowstone National Park," he said. "Try to initiate a supervolcanic eruption." He looked from me to the Russian. "The truth is, I've done some research since the Prophet first contacted me, and we probably need to set off two or three supervolcanoes across the planet in order to accomplish much, but this one act will force the world to acknowledge the severity of the problem and follow our lead." He sighed. "Of course, the Church will never get credit for our work." He shrugged. "That's the way it always goes."

At this point, the Russian man finally began to speak, though I had to ask him to repeat himself and clarify various points several times before I understood the plan. An eruption in Yellowstone would cover most of Wyoming, Montana, Idaho,

Colorado…and Utah in one to three meters of ash. Sulfuric gas would mix with water and create aerosols which would significantly cool the atmosphere.

Even a normal volcano, if its eruption was large enough, could cool the Earth by a degree or two, for at least a couple of years. A supervolcanic eruption would be hundreds of times larger, and though the cooling effect it created would also be temporary, it might be enough to give people a chance to take other measures which could finally turn runaway global warming around. For his part, the Russian assured me his government was fully, if unofficially, behind the plan.

"But how many people is this going to kill?" I asked, dumbfounded at the outrageous proposal I was hearing.

The Russian shrugged. "90,000 in the first few minutes," he said. "Several million more over the next few weeks. Depends on how long the eruption continues."

I closed my eyes and shook my head.

"Elder Olson," President Carruthers said carefully, "you do understand that killing twenty million people is the *best* outcome. If we don't stop global warming, *billions* of people are going to die."

"But…"

"And that will be twenty million fewer people driving cars and using electricity," the president continued. "The Russians are also working on biological agents that will target specific ethnic groups in China and India, but that's trickier."

"Need-to-know," the Russian man said, a bit irritated.

I stared at him. Then I cocked my head. Even in this upscale building, I could still hear music from a neighboring apartment. Sekret, it sounded like. For a brief second, part of me wondered if I was being filmed, if this was some sort of Russian prank show. Or some bizarre Abrahamic test before extending my mission three extra months and calling me to be the new AP. But the tension in the air told me this was all really happening. "But Utah," I said. "Idaho…"

The president nodded gravely. "The Prophet understands. It's all part of Heavenly Father's plan. Just as Jesus Christ was sacrificed to save the souls of all mankind, Mormons are the sacrifice to save humanity itself."

My heart was beating so hard it hurt. I put my hand on my chest. I wanted Elder Miller. I felt so alive when he was inside me. I wanted to go to a banya with him on a day that wasn't Preparation Day. I wanted to eat borscht together and then watch his pink urine fill a cup before he handed it to me.

I wanted everything we did to be okay.

But how could it be? Why was I suddenly afraid of sinning *now*?

"A few members in these areas will make it through because of their food storage," the president went on. "And eventually, survivors will gather in Jackson County, Missouri, as foretold by prophecy."

I stared at the floor, remembering how Brigham Young had said he'd rather be dead than face having to live the law of polygamy.

"Elder Olson," President Carruthers continued, "once you acquire the nuclear weapons, you'll direct them to a place this gentleman will tell you about. Then your part will be done. You can finish the last few days of your mission a proud man."

"And then go home to Salt Lake."

President Carruthers glanced at the Russian man. "I can give you an extension for one transfer," the president offered.

"So I can survive murdering everyone I know and love."

Everyone but Teancum. Oh my heck. What was I going to tell Teancum? Perhaps I should leave the Church right this minute and not do this terrible thing. I should go public and warn people what was being planned.

As if anyone would believe me. I knew what would happen if I said no.

Teancum would never see *me* again.

The president rubbed his hands together. "Well, I'll leave your departure date up to you," he said. "Of course, there will probably be some restrictions on air traffic after…" He wiped his forehead, and for the first time, I wondered if he was going to tell his three grown children in Utah to evacuate. Or if he was willing to sacrifice them as well.

President Carruthers took a deep breath, smiled, and extended the official offer. "Will you accept the Prophet's call to serve?"

I was silent a long moment, staring at the moisture on the president's forehead. I remembered a pivotal scene from *Total Recall*. My parents had always let me watch R-rated movies.

And look where that had gotten me.

"Do you understand what the Lord expects of you, Elder?"

Even with liberal parents, I'd made a lifetime of sacrifices to be a faithful Mormon, but even that hadn't made me a good person. Homosexuality was next to murder. Why not go the next step and make just one more sacrifice for the Lord? After all, I was damned to Outer Darkness anyway. I turned to look at the Russian man.

"Elder?"

"*Ya ponimayu,*" I said heavily.

The president and the Russian stood, smiling grimly, and offered their hands. I shook them both listlessly.

I wasn't even allowed to go back to my apartment to say anything to Elder Miller. The Russian man dropped me off with directions which I followed in a daze, a suitcase full of cash in one hand and instructions on how to wire the balance once the weapons were secured.

I felt the way I had my first few days in Russia, when I understood nothing, when I felt I was walking through air as thick as molasses, trying to run in a dream but unable to lift my feet. Suffocated by my ignorance.

Three days before my two years were up, I walked back to my apartment. It looked dirtier than it had before.

"Oh my god!" Elder Miller shouted, running over and squeezing me tightly. The other two elders looked on disapprovingly, either for the disrespectful words my companion had uttered or merely for the fact that we were hugging. The district leader demanded an explanation, though surely the president had made up some story for everyone already. I led Elder Miller to our bedroom and closed the door, and we began kissing in a wild frenzy.

"I thought I was never going to see you again," he said, wiping his eyes. "Why did you leave without saying goodbye?"

I looked at him and started crying, overcome by the first emotions I'd felt in days. How could I tell him I'd just arranged to kill his entire family and those of all his friends? Why hadn't I asked the Russian mafia to kill me? Why hadn't I simply jumped into the Moskva River by myself? Looking into my companion's eyes, I suddenly remembered that Laban wasn't the only problematic character in the Book of Mormon.

While Teancum was a hero, he was only a hero because he'd successfully killed Amalickiah and Ammoron, who themselves were the cause of so much death and suffering. Nephi was a murderer. Teancum was a murderer. I almost laughed, realizing that Laban was the one bad guy who'd never murdered anyone. Until I came along.

"Talk to me," Elder Miller pleaded.

I pulled him onto the bed beside me and held his hand. Should I tell him I'd also just destroyed the Church we both loved? Somehow, knowing there were no more temple recommend interviews in my future didn't make me feel any freer. I kept looking into Miller's trusting eyes and felt more pain than I had ever thought possible. How did Nephi ever look his wife in the face after what he'd done? How did he even manage to look himself in the mirror?

Perhaps it was easier to follow the Lord's commandments before there were mirrors.

For the first time, I wondered if Jesus had chosen death not only to atone for humanity's sins but also for his own, in helping create a world full of misery for so many people in the first place. Perhaps I could ask Teancum to kill me. It would be an act of compassion on his part. And I knew he loved me enough to do it. But the last thing I wanted was to turn him into a murderer, too.

"Laban…"

I leaned over and kissed Elder Miller on the forehead. "We're leaving tonight," I said. "I have connections. I can get us both jobs, maybe somewhere down in Kazan where nobody knows us."

"I don't understand."

I kissed my companion first on both cheeks and next on the lips. Then I told him everything. It was harder than any confession I'd ever had to give to my bishops back home. Elder Miller was staring at the floor when I finished, and I wondered if we were finished, too.

"When we made our vows in the temple," he said softly, "we promised to give up everything. I guess this is everything."

Did "everything" include "us"? I felt my hands trembling. Why I should regret the loss of one relationship when I'd just arranged to destroy millions of others, I didn't know. But the fact that I did made me feel like a piece of shit.

Jesus had to shit, didn't he?

Elder Miller reached over and began unknotting my tie. He gently undressed me, gave me his cum and tea, and then "returned" my head before I threw my garments back on and headed to the bathroom. The district leader demanded again to know more details about my absence, and I closed the bedroom door in his face. He kept knocking for another half hour as Elder Miller and I lay together in bed.

It occurred to me I'd never wondered before whatever became of Laban's widow after God ordered her husband's murder.

Did Judas leave behind someone he loved?

Elder Miller and I would have to change our names, I realized, suddenly feeling melancholy. And we certainly wouldn't be using the new names we'd been given the first time we went through the temple. Nothing scriptural in any way. My companion rested his head on my shoulder, and I put my hand on his chest.

After it was clear the other elders had finally gone to sleep, my companion and I packed our clothes and crept quietly out of the apartment.

We'd found low-level jobs and an apartment in Kazan by the time ash started falling in Salt Lake, but by then the honeymoon was already long over.

Clear-Cutting the Garden of Eden

"Solidarity Hall, this is Charlene. How may I help you?" Charlene clicked Delete on an email that had come in asking her boss to sign a petition encouraging Bernie Sanders to run as an Independent if he didn't win the Democratic nomination. No one in the office considered Sanders a "real" socialist.

Charlene liked him but now that his chances seemed slim, she was thinking of voting for Jill Stein of the Green Party in the fall. No one in the office approved of her, either.

"Hi, Charlene," said a female voice on the other end of the line, "is Beth in?"

Charlene turned to look toward the back of the Hall. She could see Beth at her desk through the window in the Bold Women office. Beth had grown up Presbyterian but was now an activist for atheists in addition to her work for women. She was living with a FTM trans whom Charlene had only met once. Beth herself had five dark hairs growing from her chin. They were so evenly spaced that Charlene often wondered if they were implants.

From her vantage point at the front desk, Charlene could also look through a second window past Beth's office to Tamara's office behind it. Tamara was Jewish, married with two children, and heavily involved in efforts to stop military funding for Israel. By glancing upward, Charlene could see through the large window into Andrea's office on the mezzanine, like a DJ booth overlooking a dance floor. Charlene still hadn't figured out Andrea's sexual orientation or marital status. Not that it mattered. She wasn't here to date.

Charlene wasn't able to see upstairs into Select Socialist's offices, but the three or four staff members there came down to the main floor several times throughout the day, making it easy enough to know if they were in or not. Callers only asked for a handful of people, so for the most part, Charlene could tell after a quick survey if the requested person was in and if they were busy.

"Yes, Beth's here," Charlene replied. "Can I tell her who's calling?"

"It's Maribel, about the rally on Sunday."

Charlene pressed the Hold button, hit the Intercom button, and then dialed the two-digit extension for Beth. When Beth picked up, Charlene explained who was calling, and Beth took over. Once Charlene saw the green blinking light turn red on her phone, she hung up.

Charlene had only been working at Solidarity Hall a little over five weeks, just filling in for Nara who was out recovering from gall bladder surgery. She'd met Nara on the bus one day in south Sacramento, when Charlene had been heading downtown to run an errand near the capitol.

Nara had said a few friendly words and then started right into a spiel about Bold Women. Charlene hadn't been impressed. She felt she was listening to a Mormon missionary again, like the time she and her family had converted eight years ago when Charlene was fourteen.

But Nara had continued to talk to Charlene every time they ran into each other, regularly as it seemed they both often ended up at the library on Saturdays. Then one day Nara handed her a gift. A package of baby diapers. Charlene could hardly have been five months pregnant at the time. She took the package and started crying.

"What's wrong?" Nara asked. "Did I make the wrong assumption? I'm so sorry."

Charlene shook her head. "It's just the first time anyone has ever done something nice for my baby."

Charlene looked toward the women's section of books along the wall. On the top shelf was a bronze figurine of a female worker carrying a hoe in one hand and a lamp in the other. The lamp she was carrying had a light bulb that worked as a real lamp. Over to the side was a poster showing an elderly woman's face with the quote "Women will lead the revolution" printed over it.

Charlene had taken the temp job here not only because she needed money but also out of a vague hope she'd figure out some way to protest effectively what had happened to her. Should she print flyers and send them to every address on the ward roster? Should she spray paint a slogan on the side of the stake center? Nothing appropriate had occurred to her yet.

Charlene turned back to her computer. She was doing some research for an article Beth was writing on MTF trans women. When she'd first taken the temp job, Charlene had expected to mostly be answering phones and responding to emails. But the Hall probably didn't receive more than one call an hour. She was also responsible for the leftist/feminist bookstore, but only three or four people came in to browse per week.

Mostly, she did "projects" for her two bosses. Beth from Bold Women had Charlene from 10:00 until 2:00, and then Select Socialist had her from 2:30 until 6:30.

It was surprisingly demanding work for minimum wage, but when Charlene had sent Nara a card a few days after her surgery, she'd written, "Get well soon. But not too soon," and had drawn a Smiley Face beneath it.

Charlene felt good to finally have a job. When she'd moved back home, she hadn't even enrolled at the local university. She just sat on the back patio at her parents' house and stared at the blue oak and black walnut in the yard, trying to figure out what to do with her life. She'd look at the trees, so beautiful in their majesty, and caress her abdomen, wondering how anything could ever truly be wrong in a world full of trees.

Charlene found some articles on TERFs, trans exclusionary radical feminists. The idea of excluding people for being different irritated her to no end. Then she found some articles on MTF activists in Brazil, India, and South Africa. She made some notes and forwarded all the relevant links to Beth. Then she had to add three new people to both the Bold Women and Select Socialist mailing lists.

They'd signed up at a minor event yesterday, but one of the email addresses was scribbled in such a messy hand that Charlene couldn't make out two of the letters. She made her best guess and then entered a note about other possibilities, so they could keep trying if the first email didn't go through.

"You're looking good, Charlene." Charlene looked up and saw Ellen coming through the front door. In her early forties and walking with a limp, she was the editor for the bi-monthly newspaper Select Socialist put out, a rather pretty woman with flawless skin and soft, blond hair. Ellen leaned over the desk and tried to give Charlene a kiss. Charlene pulled back.

"Please, Ellen."

"You're going to be having that baby any day now," Ellen said, "and I need to know we're a couple before that."

"And I need you to stop forcing yourself on me like my rapist did."

Ellen looked at her, muttered "Mood swings again," and headed to the door leading upstairs.

Charlene took a deep breath and started her next project, making an inventory of all the movies in the Bold Women library. Charlene had done so many once-a-year projects over the past few weeks that she had begun to wonder if Nara was a very good employee, or if her bosses were just taking advantage of her, knowing she wouldn't be around long enough to burn out. She'd stood on top of a stepladder in a cramped closet and gone through shelf after shelf of heavy banners, sorting them by topic and withdrawing those no longer relevant.

"Fossil Fuel Divestment Now" was still good, but the Hall didn't need an "End the Cuba Embargo" sign or a Gay Pride banner dated from 1981. Had no one looked at all the banners in thirty-five years? Charlene had also gone through a huge closet full of protest signs in the alley, sorting them according to topic as well—workers' rights, women's rights, immigrant rights, abortion rights.

The abortion signs always made her wonder if she'd made the right decision.

She wasn't going to report the rape at first, too confused and afraid. J Golden had even kept his garments on during the act. But once she realized she had the man's DNA replicating inside her, she went to the Title IX office on the Brigham Young campus. And was promptly investigated for breaking the Honor Code by leading her fellow student on. "You must have been drinking," the investigator said.

"I've never had so much as a sip of alcohol," Charlene insisted.

"You must have been wearing something suggestive," the investigator continued.

"I was still in my church dress," Charlene replied. "J Golden was walking me home from church and forced himself inside." He was the second counselor in her ward bishopric, a senior at BYU studying marketing.

"Well, you must have done *something* to encourage him," the woman went on. "Good priesthood holders just don't do things like that."

Charlene had almost blurted out that as a lesbian, it was unlikely she'd given off any "vibes" to the man, but she knew she was in enough trouble as it was.

"In any event," the investigator said, "we can't very well have an unwed mother at BYU. We must avoid the appearance of evil." And within three days, Charlene was expelled, two weeks before the end of her junior year. She didn't even get to take her Economic Botany or Plant Pathogens or any other finals. Thank goodness her parents in Sacramento had taken her back in, despite the scandal.

It didn't always work that way. But then, her parents were the kind of "hip" folks who had replaced the picket fence around their front yard with one made of headboards and footboards from old iron bed frames.

Of course, they still wouldn't drink tea. And even chocolate had caffeine, so that was off limits, too. Which had turned out okay since Charlene had been gaining far too much weight as it was.

Charlene looked up from the various movie titles and nodded at the middle-aged black man who came through the front door of the Hall. Pete lived in the neighborhood and strolled in three or four times a day for free coffee. He waved at her and walked straight to the pot, pouring the last of the liquid into a paper cup.

Blind in one eye, he spilled half the sugar from his packet onto the floor. Charlene walked over with a smile and began grinding more beans so she could make a fresh pot for the rest of the staff who usually came in later.

What would J Golden think if he knew what the mother of his child was doing right now?

He wouldn't care one way or the other, Charlene knew. J Golden had erased her completely from his memory. He could have shot his semen into a Kleenex for all the difference it made to him.

A moment later, Pete's friend Jesset came through the front door. He spent the entire day walking up and down the block, passing back and forth in front of the Hall window three dozen times. After pouring himself a cup of the fresh coffee, he smiled and said, "I'll put some money in the donation jar for you guys. $500."

"That's very generous," Charlene replied.

"No, that's not enough," Jesset corrected himself. "I'll put in $1000." He took another sip. "No. $10,000."

"Whatever you can spare," Charlene said.

He cocked his head twice, his usual tic after a few sips of coffee, and Pete handed him a pack of sugar, which he declined.

Charlene heard a fax come in and walked to the back of the building, trying to keep an eye on what was going on up front. As if anyone were going to rush in and steal a handful of socialist books to sell alongside fake Rolexes and pirated CDs. The fax was some kind of finance report for Tamara. Charlene put it in her mailbox, singing softly to herself. "Please, Mr. Postman."

"Did you say something?" asked Beth, stepping out of her office.

"Just talking to myself," Charlene replied. "I read somewhere that was a sign of intelligence." She paused and her brows furrowed. "Or was that insanity?" She paused again and rubbed her chin. "It was something that starts with an I."

Beth looked at her blankly until Charlene smiled. Then her boss put a hand on her chest. "You worry me sometimes, Charlene."

Beth went back into her office and Charlene looked at her watch. It was only 1:15 and she was already tired. Thank goodness it was Friday.

No. Thank God it was Friday. She could say that now.

Charlene went to church every Sunday with her parents, a condition for being allowed to live at home. Most of the members of her ward were polite enough, but somehow everyone still knew what had happened, and they blamed her for it. She overheard one woman in the bathroom tell another she thought Charlene had felt guilty for the premarital sex she'd obviously willingly participated in and so had lied about it.

But even aside from all that, Charlene was now painfully aware of how men ran the whole show. A completely male hierarchy which routinely ignored the needs of girls and women. It started with taking money the Young Women raised at bake sales and diverting it to the Scouting program, a priority which only grew worse as the girls developed into women. There was the fact that Heavenly Father was spelled with capital letters while in most official documents, heavenly mother was in lowercase.

Once, during Sacrament meeting, the bishop said, "I wouldn't be anything at all in this Church if it wasn't for the help I get from my little wife." Then he'd chuckled condescendingly.

There was also the problem that 99% of the stories taught from the scriptures were about men. Even 90% of the stories from Church history. And the ones which did mention women either described them as harlots or pointed out how faithful they were in following the men. Charlene hated the whole experience of being in church. Especially the way Brother Hill, the second counselor in the bishopric, always kept looking at her breasts.

What was it about second counselors?

Charlene worked on the inventory a while longer. Almost all the movies were on VHS. Who even watched those anymore?

Two of the tapes unbelievably were in Beta format. Only a handful were on DVD, and nothing on Blu-ray. Charlene finally grew tired and walked back to her desk, rubbing the small of her back with her hand. Her ankles were swollen, her feet straining to escape the confines of her shoes, and she'd already made three trips to the ladies' room since she began the day's shift.

When she'd first started temping, she'd been asked to help set up tables for a movie night. Some documentary on the Minneapolis truck strikes of 1934. And she'd had to stand for hours each day as she sorted through hundreds and hundreds of documents, perhaps a couple thousand sheets of paper, about the campaign Bold Women had waged to free a local African American woman from jail. She'd shot her ex-husband in the foot when he violated his restraining order and broken into her house, threatening her with a knife. She'd been sentenced to twenty years.

But after constant pressure from Bold Women and other groups, she'd finally been released, just a few weeks before Charlene took the front desk job. Another project was to put everything from that campaign in chronological order and make three piles of documents, one for Bold Women, one for the library at California State University, and one for the woman herself. The first and last piles had to be put in plastic page protectors. The library just wanted the plain box of papers.

Charlene was way too pregnant to do anything that physical now. These past few weeks, she'd gained five pounds, in addition to all the weight she'd already put on, in a month when most pregnant women gained almost nothing. How much was her baby going to weigh? She hoped it looked just like J Golden. Maybe she should name it after him and post pictures on Facebook. Some of her friends knew some of his.

She wanted to shoot J Golden in the foot.

Of course, she did want to be a mother, and as a lesbian, her only other options would be to have sex with a different man, willingly, do in vitro fertilization, or hire a surrogate. Maybe it was all for the best. Now she'd never have to touch another man the rest of her life. No temple marriage for her. Upsetting for her parents, unfortunately, who'd always had such high hopes.

Charlene had read the Book of Mormon from cover to cover before being baptized. She'd been the best student in Seminary. She'd baked cookies for her mother's Visiting Teachers and her father's Home Teachers. She'd volunteered along with the other Laurels to serve food at important business dinners for the stake president's firm.

Charlene wondered if she should lose her virginity to Ellen. Naturally, everyone at church thought she'd already lost it, but she was sure sex only counted if it was with a woman. On purpose.

She wasn't the used piece of chewing gum she was taught about in Young Women.

But did that make her a virgin mother instead? Brigham Young had insisted that Heavenly Father had physical intercourse with Mary to impregnate her with the future messiah. Charlene thought about the guys back in Provo who'd asked her to suck their dicks or let them do anal sex to her, saying if it wasn't "real" sex it didn't count, and they could still marry in the temple later when they found the right girl.

One guy had even suggested that if Charlene let him have sex with her while she was menstruating, he could even enter her vagina and it wouldn't count. He'd pronounced vagina as "vaghenah." He'd gone on to talk about how a woman's period provided "Nature's lubrication." Charlene had turned around and walked off.

Charlene leaned over to pick up a piece of debris from the Hall floor. It was a serious mistake, as she was barely able to stand back up. She breathed deeply and slowly for a minute and made it the rest of the way to her desk. There were a couple of new emails, one inviting Bold Women to participate in an emergency rally Saturday about a proposal the city council was considering. Any new events coming up in the next few days always had to be forwarded immediately to Beth for a quick appraisal.

There was also an email from a member asking about the upcoming mobilization. Once a month, Bold Women members went door to door in poor neighborhoods, trying to spread the word. Since Charlene knew all the details for the "mobe," she responded to the email herself. Just as she hit Send, another email came in, this one from Socialist Jesus, advertising a religious service in Los Angeles in two weeks. Charlene hit Delete. Beth would not be attending.

Charlene had planned to serve a mission for the Church when she graduated, hoping that another eighteen months of total dedication to the Lord would finally put a stop to all those forbidden sexual feelings. She could probably even have gotten away with serving a second mission if she had to. No one ever urged her to get married because she had so many freckles and abnormally large nostrils. She was clearly a "sweet spirit" no one would ever ask.

Of course, Ellen had asked her. Charlene thought about marrying the woman right outside the ward chapel. Make a statement. Even if they divorced six months later. Maybe they could do it during ward conference. Maybe she could post something online.

"J Golden was so bad at sex he turned me into a lesbian."

Charlene pulled up her list of media contacts. Next Saturday night, Bold Women was hosting a planning meeting to decide what kind of activism they wanted to do for the remainder of the year. She had to post an invitation along with map directions on thirty different websites—neighborhood blogs, radio stations, weekly newspapers, Facebook. She'd done most of it the day before but still had three websites left to visit. She finished with two minutes to spare before lunchtime.

"2:00!" Beth shouted, coming out of her office. Soon, everyone in the building was downstairs, warming food in the kitchen and taking their places at the folding tables. Four long tables were routinely set up in a square, and the communal lunch was a mandatory activity. It built solidarity. Charlene grabbed her tuna sandwich from the fridge and took a seat.

"Who's coming to the May Day rally on Sunday?" Tamara asked, stabbing her fork into a spinach salad. Seeing the sliced boiled eggs made Charlene a little nauseated.

"Maribel and I are bringing the card tables and books," said Beth. She was eating leftover spaghetti from home. Charlene moved a seat farther away from the tomato sauce.

"Nara said she'll try to be there," Ellen said. "She's feeling much better. She'll probably be back to work soon." Ellen gave Charlene an intense stare.

"I'll be at church with my family." Charlene shrugged. Even the tuna fish didn't taste very good today.

"Charlene, you can't raise your son Mormon." Ellen pointed a finger at her. "You need to get out of that house right now. It'll only be harder once the baby's born."

"I can't afford to live on my own."

"You can't afford to stay in that oppressive religion."

Beth and Tamara started their own conversation about an upcoming forum on raising the federal minimum wage. Andrea and Billy, a volunteer for SS, started talking about movies. Billy was a film buff, just turned eighteen, with a trim beard and long-sleeved shirts that didn't cover his eczema. He liked comedies.

Charlene hadn't seen a comedy in months which had made her laugh.

"Ellen, I don't want to live with you," Charlene said.

"But I can support you," Ellen replied.

Ellen had received a significant settlement after the accident which had damaged her left leg. Ten years earlier, she'd gone out on her balcony one night to look at the stars, and it had collapsed, sending her twenty-five feet to the street below. In addition to the settlement, she received a regular small income for her work on the paper.

"The last thing I want is to be a stay-at-home mom."

"So how is living with your parents going to change that?"

Charlene took another bite of her sandwich and didn't answer.

Ellen sniffed. "Well, if you *want* to raise your son in a rape culture…"

Charlene felt a wave of irritation but looked down at her sandwich and kept chewing, feeling strangely defensive. Rape was no more common among Mormons than any other group. She felt she was being attacked personally. But it wasn't as if Ellen were behaving any differently than the others. Beth might tell Andrea she'd done a poor job of cooking for the last forum. Tamara might tell Ellen she hadn't prepared her lesson for study group adequately. No one felt any reason to hold back what they were really thinking.

Charlene found it obnoxious but also mysteriously exciting. It was a bit like a wildfire burning out the undergrowth amongst the trees to make the forest healthier.

She tried to imagine everyone she knew saying what they really thought at any moment. It never happened at church. And certainly not at BYU. It only rarely happened at home. Charlene still didn't quite know how to negotiate such conversations at work.

She heard Billy make a comment about a movie he'd just watched on TV. *Nine to Five*. A film Charlene had seen twice her first year of college and enjoyed. Partly because she'd heard Lily Tomlin was a lesbian. But she could never decide if Tomlin was a role model or a degenerate temptress leading her to Outer Darkness. The woman seemed so normal. Charlene had wanted to watch the film a third time but decided it might hurt her testimony, so she'd resisted.

"I just love the ending," Billy said, "when Violet gets promoted, and Judy marries the Xerox repairman, and Doralee becomes a country and western singer."

"What about when Mr. Hart gets kidnapped by a tribe of Amazons?" asked Andrea.

"The indigenous people of Brazil are not called Amazons," Charlene said, hoping to keep Ellen from pestering her any further. It also gave her a chance to practice speaking her mind. These people didn't know everything. "My brother lived in Brazil for two years. The Indians are called Yanomami and Cashibo and dozens of other names. But they're not Amazons."

She'd thought even as a naïve college freshman that the line was an ignorant slap at native peoples. She wasn't going to be ignorant. She'd hoped to serve a mission in Thailand or Ghana and learn a little about the world.

Robert had been a bossy and petulant older brother until his mission to São Paulo. Serving mostly in small, isolated towns, the first thing he did upon returning home was take a prescription medication which killed parasites. The next morning, he deposited a bowlful of worms. He took a picture and sent it to Charlene.

"TMI, brother, TMI," Charlene had emailed back. "Will I see you here at BYU next quarter?"

He was soon in Provo, too, studying Chemistry while teaching Portuguese part-time at the Missionary Training Center for a little extra money. But when he found out what had happened to Charlene, the first thing he did was mail a box of worm-infested dog shit to J Golden. God only knew how he acquired it. He then ordered a subscription to *Big Dick* magazine for him, having it delivered to J Golden's BYU address. Robert said if BYU wouldn't expel the creep for rape, maybe they'd do it for the more serious sin of pornography.

J Golden wasn't expelled, and Robert transferred to the University of Utah.

"Oh, Charlene," said Andrea with a smile. "It's a joke. Amazons are a legendary tribe of strong women. Did you notice what the movie was about?"

Charlene frowned.

"I wish you'd join our study group," Beth said.

Charlene took another bite of her sandwich and almost gagged. The taste was really off today. She stood up and went to the sink near the coffee pot to get some water. Maybe she did need to skip church Sunday and go to the May Day rally. There was so much she wanted to understand.

Charlene asked for light duty the rest of the afternoon and was handed a box of five hundred envelopes. Sitting at the lunch table with everything spread out in front of her, she stamped each envelope first with a return address and then with the group's assigned postage number.

She used the paper-folding machine to fold five hundred full-page orange flyers advertising Select Socialist's next movie night and five hundred yellow half-sheet flyers advertising their newspaper subscription drive rates. Then she stuffed all the envelopes and took a tube of water with a small sponge on the end to dampen and seal all the envelopes.

Her only break came around ten minutes to five, when Ellen came downstairs and sat down beside her. "Look at this," she said, holding her phone in front of Charlene.

"What is it?"

"Tyler Glenn from Neon Trees."

"Who?"

"Good grief, Charlene. You at least need to learn about activists in your own religion."

"Are they Mormon environmentalists?" she asked. The idea excited her. "Do you guys work with them?"

"Oh, for crying out loud. Just look."

Charlene watched as a reasonably attractive young man with a daring haircut started singing. She gasped when the man spit on a portrait of Joseph Smith. Her eyes widened when she saw him giving himself the secret temple handshakes. It wasn't her type of music, but the refrain, "One man's trash is another man's treasure," was nevertheless haunting.

She wanted to do something bold. Be a Bold Woman.

"Thanks, Ellen." Charlene put her hand on Ellen's arm, and the woman smiled. Then Charlene returned to her work, finishing around 6:20.

She put the chain back around the double doors leading to the alley, cleaned the coffee pot, drew the curtains closed over the front windows, and carried the sandwich board in from the sidewalk. She turned off the Open sign, locked the front door, and turned off all but one light. Almost everyone had already left the building except for Beth downstairs and Andrea upstairs. They all exited from the back door, and Charlene headed home for the evening.

Waiting for the bus, Charlene read her latest text. Ellen wanted to know if she could treat Charlene to dinner. She put the phone back in her purse.

Charlene ate with her parents at the kitchen table as she did every night. They talked about Dolly Parton's upcoming concert tour. Charlene thought about Amazons. She plopped into bed before 9:00, while her parents were still watching a rerun of *Gilmore Girls*.

She wasn't sure entitlement counted as empowerment.

Saturday morning, Charlene wanted to sleep in late, but the baby was pressing on her bladder. Once up, though, she sat on the patio and looked out at the blue oak and black walnut in the back yard for a couple of hours. The light breeze felt so good in the shade. And the trees were always beautiful.

Maybe she should try to finish her degree. The American Chestnut Foundation was working to develop a hardier, disease-resistant tree. Her mom could help babysit while she was in class, as long as Charlene didn't mind having a religious son.

Of course, her parents were decent, so her son might turn out to be a good Mormon, too. She didn't want to throw the baby out with the bathwater. Or was that baptismal font water? Charlene tried calling Nara, but when the phone went instead to voice mail, she hung up. She read a booklet Beth had given her on strategies to fight domestic violence and dozed on the lawn chair.

When it was time for lunch, she took an aspirin for her back. She was generally good with pain, hadn't even cried out during the assault last year or that time two girls had beaten her in the high school bathroom a few years before that. She hoped to get through the fast-approaching delivery without any medication. She reread the booklet, wanting to fully understand it.

After a relaxing, peaceful day, when the world almost seemed good, it was time for dinner. Charlene's mom served sloppy joes, Charlene's favorite comfort food. They were all supposed to be fasting, but her parents had insisted she eat on fast days, and they ate with her to ensure she didn't feel sinful for doing so. She took a quick bite of the tempting meal the moment her father offered the blessing. Thank God it tasted okay.

"From the look of things," her mother said, "you don't have many comfortable days left." She laughed. "But at least you'll probably get flowers a week from tomorrow for being the newest mother in the ward."

"I can hardly wait." Charlene almost added, "Kind of makes it all worth it," but stopped herself in time. Charlene's father would want to give the baby a name and a blessing in a few weeks, and then her son's name would be on official Church records for the rest of his life, whether he was ever baptized or not. Whether he was baptized and then resigned or not.

Perhaps she should move in with Ellen, just for a little while. Too bad Nara wasn't a lesbian. Not that there was anything wrong with platonic roommates, of course. It worked in *New Girl*.

After dinner, they all retired to the living room, her parents on the sofa and Charlene in the easy chair. Her father waved the remote in the air and grinned. "Anyone up for 'LDS or Gentile'?"

It was a game Charlene and her father sometimes played, despite her mother finding it disrespectful. The game was based on an episode of *The Big Bang Theory* where Howard teases his friend Raj by telling the rest of the gang various quotes and asking if Raj said it to his girlfriend or to his dog. "Emily or Cinnamon: How can such a little girl eat such a big steak?"

Charlene's father started something similar after hearing Charlene make a snide remark one day while her parents were watching General Conference reruns. He'd ask Charlene to go to the kitchen where she couldn't see the TV screen, and he'd turn to a lecture channel. It could be a snippet from a conference or some other Mormon talk. Or it might be someone speaking at the public library about Laura Ingalls Wilder, or a scientist talking about the need to provide vertical evacuation options for coastal communities vulnerable to tsunami, or even a megachurch preacher talking about the greatness of God. Often, her father would lower the volume so Charlene couldn't make out the actual words, only hear the speech pattern itself.

Charlene struggled out of the easy chair now and waddled back to the kitchen. She listened as her father switched to three different stations, as if he thought "shuffling the cards" would make any difference. Soon, she heard a woman talking about her PhD and the need for women to get an education. Not a particularly Mormon topic, but the speaker had that typical Mormon cadence. Slow, deliberate, with a lack of enthusiasm, a specific type of pause, a unique lilt. Was it Emily or Cinnamon?

It was a tough call, but Charlene finally said, "LDS," and walked back into the living room. Her father was watching the BYU channel. Mormon speech patterns were unmistakable.

"Really, Dad?" Charlene asked. "BYU when I'm nine months pregnant? Maybe we should put the game on hiatus for a while."

"Oops. Sorry." He and Charlene's mother exchanged glances and then her father switched to *Miss Congeniality* on TBS just a few minutes into the movie. While Charlene appreciated the more secular topic, she wished she'd borrowed a DVD from the Bold Women library instead to watch sometime over the weekend. *Suffragette* or *Made in Dagenham* or *North Country* or any of the other films on important moments in the history of women's rights she needed to learn about. She tried to watch the familiar story with her parents but quickly grew annoyed because of the incessant commercial breaks. Her parents owned the flippin' DVD. Why didn't they just put the damn disk in and watch the movie without advertising?

"I'm heading to bed," Charlene announced an hour in.

"So early?"

"Hormones," Charlene explained. It was a great answer any time she felt irritable. Although it irked her to no end when Ellen said it.

Her mother stood up and hugged Charlene tightly, kissing her on the forehead. "Everything will be okay," she whispered. "I promise."

Charlene forced a smile and went to her room. She debated whether to pray but then read some poems by Maya Angelou and turned out the light.

She awoke early on Sunday morning, her back hurting more than the day before. She felt a little off and skipped breakfast despite her mother's wagging finger. She fixed her hair and make-up and put on the only dress which still fit. This Fast Sunday she would bear her testimony. Not of the gospel but of her love for her parents. It was the least she could do to pay them back. But she might throw in a socialist point or two as well. The Church did have a socialist history, after all, no matter how hard they tried to hide it now.

"You sit in the front seat, dear," her mother said, helping her into her father's Buick. Her mother sat in the back seat. The chapel was a few miles away, and they took the highway for a bit. Charlene watched as a fuel truck rolled past, followed by three cars with unidentifiable paint jobs.

Car colors were determined by marketing and varied every few years. Vehicles now didn't even have shades she could recognize. They were a blend of green and gray, or blue and green and maybe brown, or combinations she couldn't begin to identify. What kind of world was it when even colors were too hard to understand? Maybe she'd name her son John, or David. Something simple. Not Joseph.

Another eighteen-wheeler rushed by, her father always a slow driver. The truck had a sign reading "Edensaw" on the side. Charlene realized the vehicle was carrying lumber, and she slapped the side of her face. The company was actually *boasting* about cutting down trees in idyllic forests as if that were a selling point.

Soon they arrived at the meetinghouse, and Charlene urged her parents to go in ahead of her. She walked slowly, feeling enormous. Relief Society would meet first today, followed by Gospel Doctrine, and finally by Fast and Testimony meeting. Charlene had peed right before leaving the house but still felt the need to stop in the bathroom before joining her mother.

Then just as she sat down, she heard a rush of fluid splashing into the toilet. Her water had broken. She almost laughed, thinking of the convenience of the location. Heavenly Father was protecting his property from being soiled unnecessarily. It was a miracle.

Tender mercies.

Then an idea occurred to her. Charlene had heard that a woman's first labor could last several hours, even more than a day. If that were the case, then there'd be no harm in attending her meetings. Her parents could casually take her to the hospital afterwards. But her mother had always recounted how she had given birth quickly to her two children, and Charlene realized she had a timeline of three hours to have her baby on church grounds. She wasn't sure why, but it seemed the perfect way to protest the official attitude toward women.

The first contraction came shortly after Sister Jenkins gave the opening prayer before the Relief Society lesson. Charlene wanted to grunt, but she'd learned long ago to bear regular muscle cramps without making a sound, even if as a child she'd always cried out in pain. She could do this. By the end of Sunday School, the contractions were about six minutes apart. She wondered if she should call Ellen. Both Bold Women and Select Socialist liked to film every political protest.

"Are you okay?" her mother asked as they moved slowly toward the chapel for the last meeting. "You're sweating quite a lot."

"I'm fine," Charlene returned, her jaw clenched so tightly she could barely understand her own answer. Charlene's mom frowned, but they kept walking.

"Perhaps we should sit in back near the door," her father suggested.

Charlene shook her head. "Front row," she managed. "Want to bear my testimony today."

They all moved slowly to the front of the chapel and sat in the middle of the pew, right in front of the podium. The meeting began as usual with an opening hymn. "The Spirit of God like a fire is burning," Charlene sang from memory. She was going to have a baby today. Her son was being born on May Day. He might grow up to be a great labor leader.

Charlene had three contractions during the interminable passing of the sacrament and had to fight to keep herself silent during the only quiet part of the entire three hours of services. She made it through five testimonies as well, even one by Sister Sorenson detailing how each individual flower in her garden taught her a different spiritual lesson.

Something she normally might agree with but which today made her feel pissy. Finally, Charlene felt something different and could tell the time had come. At the next awful contraction, she screamed both in physical pain and emotional relief that she was now going to have her moment. She kicked off her shoes and lay down on the carpet in front of the podium.

Everyone stopped in their tracks like statues, as if turned to salt for looking the wrong way. Charlene screamed again, probably louder than was necessary, and this time her mother dropped to the floor at her feet. "Oh my God!" Charlene heard her mother shout, feeling a perverse pleasure at the offending words. "She's crowning! I need some help here!"

Charlene had no idea if parents were ushering their children back into the lobby to spare them the experience, but she knew she had the attention of at least a couple of dozen worshippers, and that would do. She wanted to cry out, "This is my rapist's baby!" but of course everyone already knew of the accusation. Announcement or not, they'd remember the circumstances of the conception every time they remembered the birth.

Though everyone seemed to forget that Mary had been raped.

Charlene felt a fleeting thrill as she thought of befouling both the chapel and anyone who pitched in to help her, but it was too hard to feel anything other than distress. She could see people frantically trying to find someone who knew what to do, and she was horrified when the second counselor kneeled in front of her.

"I'm an Eagle Scout," Brother Hill told everyone. "Always prepared for emergencies. The priesthood to the rescue!" He nodded toward the others as if humbly accepting an award.

Charlene wanted to tell him to get away from her, that she'd just pop out the baby on her own and take her chances, but she could hardly think anymore. All she knew was that she seemed to be defecating a watermelon. She'd never imagined the degree of desperation she would feel.

"Ellen!" she cried out. "Nara!"

Everyone looked about in confusion. Charlene watched Brother Hill on his knees in front of her, her dress up above her waist, her legs spread. She couldn't tell if he was looking at the baby's head or…

She felt a hand touching her where there was no need to touch. Her eyes locked onto the counselor's as he kept rubbing her pubic hair. He was looking into her open legs, taking everything in. Oh my God, Charlene thought, what was happening? She wanted Beth. She wanted Tamara. She wanted Andrea.

She wanted her mama. Where was her mama? Everyone seemed to have moved farther away. "Oh, God!"

Charlene watched in horror as Brother Hill squeezed in closer. "I'm glad you don't shave," he whispered. She could see J Golden's face in front of her. Please, Heavenly Father, she begged, don't let the baby look like J Golden. The pain was overwhelming and she screamed again.

The counselor licked his lips and grinned.

The Assimilation of Hector Garcia

My alarm rang and I reached over to switch it off. As I fell back onto my pillow, I glanced at the empty spot beside me in bed. I missed Hector. But he'd be back in Boise in a few days after a week of fun with some friends down in Florida. He'd dreamed of Disneyworld and Universal Studios ever since he'd heard about them as a boy in San Antonio. My own family had made one memorable trip to Anaheim when I was eight.

I'd always thought it a special reward for being the last child in the family to be baptized—my sister had received a brand new bike the year before—but I later learned my mother had inherited a few thousand dollars when her father died, and this was the way my parents chose to spend it. In retrospect, it seemed a little frivolous, considering how my father always struggled to make ends meet, but on the other hand, it was a trip we all talked about when we got together even eighteen years later.

Back when we were still speaking, anyway.

Sunday mornings were different now that I'd left the LDS Church. No more scrambling to get ready for meetings, preparing a lesson at the last minute. Of course, I still had to get ready for work. I heated some oatmeal in the microwave, cut up a banana, and sprinkled some brown sugar over the top of the mess. Then I sprinkled a little more.

I toyed with my iPhone, but there were no new texts from Hector. The last was from yesterday evening just as I was closing up at midnight. "Love U, Alex," he said.

Hector never let one day go by without telling me he loved me. He was dancing last night with his friends at a club named Pulse. It was Latino Night. But even in the midst of all that exuberance, he found time to tell me goodnight. I'd texted a love note back and then went home and collapsed into bed.

This morning, I had the day shift, from 10:00 to 4:30. Last night, I'd had to work with Louise, a chunky woman in her forties who insisted on playing loud classic rock all evening. My ears were still ringing.

After rinsing my bowl, I jumped in the car and headed to the dreariest part of town, the only area which could support an adult video store without anyone giving a damn. I'd been working at *All My Desires* for four months, ever since I'd graduated with my MBA in Marketing.

Hector had wanted me to take a job in Chicago or New York or even Seattle or Portland, but after being excommunicated from the Church and disowned by my family for moving in with him, the only thing I wanted right now was a job where I could be free. Since I didn't know the first thing about bartending, and I didn't particularly want to bag groceries, I'd applied for the clerk position at the video store.

"You're gonna regret it," Hector said when I told him I'd been called in for an interview. He was a mechanic in a repair shop which only worked on American cars, studying on his own to add German cars to his repertoire. "We're a global society," he kept telling me. "No one is Japanese or British or Mexican anymore." He shook his head as I picked up my folder with an extra copy of my resumé.

"So what's a life without regrets?" I asked.

He gave me the finger in response. I leaned forward and took it in my mouth. He then unzipped and said, "I think you're helping me blossom as the rose." I was almost late for my interview.

I pulled up to the video store now and unlocked the door, moving quickly to turn off the alarm. Some of the nearby businesses had cracked front glass doors held together with silver duct tape. There were a couple of bars, a pawn shop, a jewelry exchange, and a thrift store spread out over a three-block area, in between the businesses which were boarded up altogether.

There was a pool hall right next door, and even a massage parlor two doors down which couldn't possibly be legit in this neighborhood. The few people on the streets looked drunk or drugged or simply destitute and homeless, mostly white but a few black and Latino. One large building was a former auto repair shop, closed long before Hector arrived in town looking for a job.

It was also boarded up, looking derelict, but nevertheless seemed to be operating as a Hispanic church, the only evidence that it was currently functional a vinyl sign tacked above the door reading "Iglesia Cristiana."

I'd served my mission in Missouri, so Hector and I could only speak to each other in English. He liked it that way. He kept saying he wanted to be a "real American," a citizen of the world, not just of Chiapas. His mother was Tzotzil and his father a Spanish merchant. They'd all converted when Hector was ten.

I checked my phone. No texts. It wasn't like Hector not to respond to my Good Morning messages. Of course, we'd never been apart before now, so what was normal? My manager didn't like employees to make personal calls while at work, and we were never allowed any internet usage while on our shifts, so that meant no email, either, even when no one else was in the store. But 4:30 wasn't a lifetime away. I'd waited to find love until I was twenty-six. I could wait a few more hours to hear Hector's voice again.

I counted "Steve," the unlocked lockbox where we stored our money. We always kept exactly $315 inside, but we were forbidden from using the word "safe" at work. Then I counted my drawer, another $200, mostly in ones and fives. I'd just finished counting and was flipping through the multitude of porn channels to make sure all the films in the booths were working properly when Tammy came through the door.

"Hi, Alex," she said. "How's it hanging?" She pushed past the swinging gate beside the counter and dropped her frayed backpack on the floor behind the glass case housing the lube and poppers. The flesh under her smallpox vaccination scar jiggled.

"To the right," I said with a nod. Then I pointed to her breasts. "How're they drooping?" Tammy was positively ancient, at least in her mid-fifties, and looked like she'd used meth at some point. She had a ring through her lower lip. When she pulled on it, one could see her horribly discolored teeth.

"Straight down, as always." She tried to lift one up, but it collapsed back immediately. "You know you're just jealous because I get propositioned more than you do." Tammy was saving up meds so when she could no longer face her chronic depression, she could swallow a dozen pills and then drive off a cliff.

We made a quick check that all the DVD covers were neatly aligned on the shelves, and then it was time to turn on the Open sign and unlock the door.

There was no sudden rush of customers. How the owner managed to keep two of us on duty during every shift, I didn't know. Some days, we barely made $60 in sales and rentals. Of course, the booths made money once people started trickling in.

"What station do you want?" Tammy asked, walking into our tiny control room where monitors displayed every part of the store. There was no one in the rental section. No one in the For Sale section. No one in the toy section. No one in the arcade.

"Do you mind if we just keep it quiet for a while?" I asked. I pointed to one of the giant fans resting atop the arcade booths. The place lacked air conditioning, and since it was mid-June, the temperature could grow pretty warm as the day progressed. "Those things are so noisy that if we turn on the radio, too, I can't hear the door chime when someone walks in."

Tammy frowned, looked at the fans, turned back to me, and shrugged. "I'm a little hung over anyway," she conceded.

"You didn't go out with Boris again, did you?" He was a regular, and though we weren't supposed to be "intimate" with any customers, Tammy couldn't resist this man fifteen years her junior, who was "almost always" clean.

"What can I say?" She shrugged. "He buys me drinks, and all I have to do is pass out for him. He likes it better that way."

I looked at the DVDs on the walls in front of me, a section for New Releases, one for MILF, and other sections for heterosexual Anal and Oral. Then there were Breasts Large and Small, Lesbian, Black, Asian, Ethnic, and Interracial. Next came sections for Amateur, Fetish, Gay, Trans, and Bisexual. These were followed by Bondage, Group, Celebrities, and something called POV.

I still had no idea what that meant. There was even some Mormon pornography—*Cum, Cum, Ye Saints*. Many of the various DVD covers were so repulsive I worried I was promoting rape culture. But since the Church condemned pornography, I couldn't stop myself from thinking these films must instead be a good thing. At least some of them. Fat, ugly, old people deserved a sex life, too, and if they could only get it vicariously, they damn well had a right to it.

It wasn't as if Mormons didn't believe in providing saving ordinances by proxy.

"Let me tell you what he did to me last night," Tammy went on.

"Oh, really, that's okay," I replied, holding up my hand.

Tammy laughed. "You're so vanilla."

Hector always said that when we had sex, we created "a vanilla latte of love." Since I'd never drunk coffee, I let myself assume that was a good thing. It sounded a bit sugary for my taste. He did have a sweet tooth, though, usually baking desserts after I cooked the main course. While we made an effort to eat our meals together, we didn't feel we had to do everything else as a couple.

Hector liked to go out dancing more than I did, while I preferred reading *The New Yorker*. What we both enjoyed most was spending a quiet evening at home watching movies. *Angels and Demons. Die Hard. The Bedroom Window*. I would sit up on the sofa and Hector would lie down with his head in my lap, my arm across his chest. Who needed anything else?

No one came in the video store for the first hour, but then two men walked in together and went directly to different parts of the floor. I motioned to Tammy to show which one I would keep an eye on, so she could track the other. My guy went to the toys, the riskiest part of my job. It was no big deal if someone stole an empty DVD case. And obviously no one was going to run off with our pinball machine.

Though sometimes when it started blaring, "Come to the Check Point!" "Come to the Check Point!" "Come to the Check Point!" over and over every three seconds, I wished someone would.

I watched as the man in his late twenties browsed the cock rings and vibrators. He looked over the party decorations, straws shaped like penises and penis-shaped cake pans. He fingered the packages containing a string of balls one could insert up one's ass, and the rubber woman's midsection sporting both vaginal and anal openings—since no other part of a woman's body was apparently necessary. He passed by the fringe for women's nipples, the one-size-fits-most women's panties, and the fur handcuffs. But he lingered too long at the dildos.

Dildos were where we lost the most money. And by "we," I meant the employees. At least once a month, someone ran off with a big purple dildo or a two-headed red dildo or something similar. If it happened on our watch, we had to pay for the missing merchandise ourselves. I walked out onto the floor. "Can I help you?" I asked.

The man looked at me, glanced down at my crotch, and then turned away. "No, I'm okay." He walked out the front door, and the other man, about the same age, suddenly seemed to lose interest in the "Bang My Tranny Ass" DVD cover he'd been studying. He left the store a moment later as well.

Soon, though, we had our first real customer. A trim elderly man came in and walked straight to the arcade. He picked the second-to-last booth on the left, the booth people always chose first. Who could ever fathom why?

I watched the monitor to see when the man put money into the machine. It took him almost ninety seconds. I was just on my way to the back with a flashlight when the light turned red over his booth door. Moans and pants began emanating from inside the enclosure.

Tammy opened her backpack and pulled out a bag of ranch-flavored Doritos. We weren't supposed to eat in sight of the customers, but I wasn't going to monitor my coworkers, too. She offered the bag to me. I shook my head and looked at the dildos.

It had been three days since I'd had Hector inside me. And he wouldn't be returning till Tuesday night, a whole two and a half days from now. I remembered the first time he'd entered me. We were the only two men who showed up to clean the men's toilets at the ward meetinghouse one Saturday. He'd called out for assistance from one of the stalls, and when I'd opened the door, his member was pointing happily at me.

I'd liked Hector since he'd moved into the ward a few months earlier, but I'd had no idea he was gay. Dangling his keychain playfully, he opened his vial of consecrated olive oil, rubbed the liquid over his dick, and then motioned for me to drop my pants.

It was awkward when folks at parties or volunteer events asked the inevitable question. "How did you guys meet?"

As the hours passed today, several more men went into the arcade. At one point, so many men were opening doors and moving to other compartments to check out their new neighbors through the glory holes, only to have those neighbors then leave for other cubicles to find better partners of their own, that I thought it would be great to set the video monitor to music emphasizing the "musical chairs" scene we witnessed every day in the control room.

Sometimes, when I went to remind someone to put more money in the machine, I could see both below and above the door that the man was fully occupied. But he had to take a break and put another dollar in the machine or leave. Those were the rules. One dollar gained him two more minutes.

"And most of these guys are married," Tammy said in disgust. "I'd never marry a man who came here."

"Isn't Boris married?" I couldn't resist asking.

"*I'm* not married to him, am I?"

I wondered if Hector was fooling around while down in Florida. Was that why he hadn't called this morning? Of course, we'd never sworn fidelity. I'd always just assumed. But it was impossible to work at a store like this and not realize that most men were pigs.

Maybe not most, but lots. Half of the guys who came here looked like cold, emotionless serial killers.

Alfred walked through the door then, his stringy white hair so greasy I expected to see thick drops falling onto the floor. Tammy pointed to me with a "you take him" signal. I waved the pot-bellied man over, and he handed me a dripping wet twenty. What in the world did these guys do with their money? I gave him two fives and ten ones in return. I wiped down the twenty, put it in the drawer, and pumped some hand sanitizer on my hands.

We went through a lot of hand sanitizer here. Even when we weren't picking up used tissues in the booths.

I sat on my stool and looked at the movie posters pasted on the walls above the DVD racks. *Fleshdance. Beverly Hills Humping.* Some of them were signed by the "stars."

A man came in to buy a glass pipe, and another man came in to buy an herbal supplement for "enhancement." The lone pill cost $8.

"That shit don't work," Tammy said after the guy left.

"How would you know?" I asked with a smile.

"I'm like the fragrance woman at the mall," she said with a shrug. "Good customer service means providing a tester." She pushed one breast up, but it fell down again immediately. She'd have probably had more success if she tried wearing a bra.

I began to wonder not only what we were teaching men to think about women, but what we were teaching women to think about women, too.

I remembered in my last Elders Quorum meeting, the subject of pornography came up. Hector had stopped attending by that point, and I'd already been working here a month. Two of the elders publicly admitted to being addicted, though I knew that in

Mormon terms, even just one look constituted addiction. But then the conversation took an odd turn. "Do you think a magazine of any kind that has a photo of a woman in a sleeveless dress is pornography?" the Elders Quorum president asked.

"Yes," most of the class murmured in response. That of course made things like the issue of *Time* featuring Laverne Cox a porn magazine. I couldn't resist smiling and feeling superior, knowing my fellow strait-laced priesthood holders were thrown into fits of lustful thoughts upon seeing someone they considered a man.

"Do you think a *woman* wearing a sleeveless dress is pornography?" the president continued.

The class nodded in agreement, and I looked about in confusion. He wasn't talking about pictures any longer.

"Do you think a woman wearing short shorts is pornography?"

The class nodded again.

"What about—?"

"Please!" one young man yelled out. He'd recently returned from his mission to Panama. He jumped up and ran out of the room. Apparently, even talk about what might constitute pornography *also* constituted pornography.

Tammy didn't look like pornography to me.

"Do you think describing a woman as pornography *is* pornography?" I said aloud. "Or just vulgar?"

"Huh?" Tammy said absentmindedly, working on her adult coloring book. She usually colored in one drawing per shift.

The front door opened, and a man pressed it firmly shut behind him. He jerked his thumb over his back. "The Baptists are out there again."

Two women and one man from a local Baptist church protested out front every Sunday after services. They stayed maybe thirty minutes and then returned home for a late lunch. We didn't get any lunch breaks here. No breaks of any kind, other than a quick run to the bathroom. Which reminded me of my full bladder.

I grabbed the bathroom key and headed down the hall of the arcade. At the end of the arcade was another hall leading off to the right, and at the end of that was the locked bathroom. We ended up giving out the key three or four times per shift. As I reached to insert the key into the lock, though, I felt something cold touch my right foot.

I looked down. Someone had urinated all over the floor in front of the bathroom door. And I realized now there was a crack in the sole of my right shoe. Urine had wicked up into my sock.

Goddammit.

Still, it wasn't as bad as the small, sticky pool of santorum I'd had to wipe up in one of the booths last week. I'd put on rubber gloves for that.

I went to the supply closet, feeling my wet sock squish about in my shoe, and pulled out a mop and bucket. Tammy was laughing as I walked back up to the front counter. "You look pissed," she said.

"Funny."

Pumping out some hand sanitizer, I waited on a middle-aged man who wanted to rent three DVDs. A picture of a shriveled old woman licking a young man's asshole was on the cover of one of them. *Grandma's Favorite Grandson.* I didn't register what was on the cover of the other two. A person became desensitized pretty quickly to this kind of stuff. I wondered if that was a good thing.

What I wanted was for gays and lesbians and queers in general to be so normal no one bothered to talk about them anymore. I wanted gay Mormons to be an everyday thing. Gay Mormon marriages. I wanted love to be so commonplace that it was no longer remarkable.

Tammy sold two half-priced DVDs to a man we had to card. I didn't even notice if the movies were gay or straight.

But I realized I didn't feel particularly free anymore, as I had at the beginning. Hadn't for some time. There was a lot to be said for rebellion and the refusal to conform. How could society ever move forward even a little without that? But I didn't want to be a rebel. I wanted to live happily ever after with Hector and the kids we planned to raise.

I wondered how we would know when we were finally assimilated into society. Checking out a DVD with a picture of a Catholic nun going down on a priest, I fantasized about kneeling across the altar from Hector in the Boise temple. Or maybe the Manhattan temple. Or the one in Chicago.

I needed to listen to Hector and start looking for a job in Marketing.

The remaining few hours of the shift dragged by with only one more incident. A thirty-something white guy tried to go in the booth of a twenty-something Latino, who openly welcomed him. We had to kick them both out.

Would Tuesday night ever come?

While Tammy counted her drawer, I wiped the glass counters with Windex. At least there was no vacuuming on the day shift. I sold a package of gummy undies and then counted my drawer while Louise counted Tammy's so she could take over for the night shift. Then Barry, a young man with long brown hair who always wore one of his two favorite death metal T-shirts, counted mine.

"Have fun, guys," Tammy said, picking up her backpack and walking out. I waved too and headed for my car.

I plopped down in the seat and breathed out heavily. Free at last. Until Wednesday morning, anyway. I turned on my phone and frowned. There were over a dozen messages and even more texts. I only had two friends after everyone at church cut me off. What the hell was going on?

Then I started reading, and sweat began to drip down my forehead and armpits. Forty-nine people had been gunned down in Orlando by a terrorist. My heart began beating faster and faster. I kept scrolling. Should I listen to voice mail first? What was the quickest way to find out what I needed to know? I rolled my window down to get some air and kept scrolling.

And there it was. A text from some number that wasn't Hector's but reading "It's Hector. Shot twice. Lost two fingers. Am okay. Luv U." Sent at 10:07 this morning.

I started crying.

I turned on the car radio and listened to a clip of a preacher in Sacramento saying he hoped someone else would "finish the job" and kill the rest of the gays. Over fifty other people had been injured by the shooter. Some had bled to death waiting for help.

Sitting there in front of the video store in a daze listening to the coverage, I watched a man walk out with a shrink-wrapped bundle of old sex magazines, it's huge $9.95 orange sticker glowing decadently in the sunshine.

I wondered if there were other kinds of pornography besides the crap we rented every day. Hector and I had watched *True Lies* the night before he left, to get him in the mood for Florida. It was a fun movie—with dozens of people slaughtered throughout the story.

Even when Jamie Lee Curtis accidentally killed a roomful of men, it was supposed to be funny. Hector and I both laughed. I turned the station and heard a reporter claim the shooting at Pulse was "the largest mass shooting in U.S. history." All I could think was that this sounded more like a challenge than a statement of fact.

Someone was going to top this.

When Hector came home after he was released from the hospital, we were going to watch a different DVD. Perhaps *Sister Act*. Hmmm. Maybe *Heaven Can Wait*. I frowned. How about *Date Night*?

Oh my God!

How would we know when murder was fully assimilated into society?

I tried calling Hector, but his personal phone wasn't working and the one he'd texted from went straight to voice mail. None of the hospitals in Orlando were giving out information. After I got back home, I turned on CNN, my phone in my hand. Despite the flurry of calls I'd received while I was at work, the phone was so lifeless now I had to keep checking to make sure it was charged.

I heated a can of creamed corn without taking my eyes off the screen. Maize was a Native American food. Given to us by the Lamanites. I took a few bites but then put the bowl away in the fridge. The news kept repeating in a loop. I finally distracted myself by sitting at my computer polishing my resumé.

But I was still able to answer Hector's call when it finally came two hours later, catching it on the first ring.

The Pro-Anti-Nephi-Lehies

"You're late, Bryce," said Don, pulling me into the apartment. "You know we like to start on time."

"Sorry." I winced. "I got off work late, and I had to shower before coming over."

Don nodded. "Well, thanks for that, anyway."

We joined David and Wayne in the living room. They were standing next to the coffee table, looking down at the latest issue of the *Ensign*. After shaking hands formally, we all sat down on the sofa, squeezing in next to each other.

"Now that we're finally all here," Don announced from the far right end of the sofa, "the Not Even Once Club will come to order." I was two guys down, sandwiched between David and Wayne. "Bryce, will you say the opening prayer?"

Lowering my head, I folded my arms and closed my eyes. "Dear Heavenly Father," I began, "thank you for this opportunity to meet and strengthen our resolve to live moral lives. Please help our activities tonight to go well and bless us with righteous girlfriends we can take to the temple. In the name of Jesus Christ. Amen." I looked up as the others did the same and unfolded their arms.

"Short and sweet," said David.

"So we can get right to business," Wayne agreed.

"I thought we changed the name of our support group," I said. "Aren't we the Pro-Anti-Nephi-Lehies now? Not Even Once is already taken."

David nodded vigorously. "And it's more in keeping with the Sons of Helaman support group," he said.

Don held up a hand. "My bad," he said. "I'll remember next Thursday."

The four of us had formed our support group three months earlier, agreeing to meet once a week. After some debate, we agreed to leave Friday and Saturday nights open for dating appropriate women, but we also wanted something immediately before the weekend so that our resolve would still be reasonably strong while we were on those dates.

"Okay." Wayne reached for his belt buckle. "Let's get started. I've still got Home Teaching to do later."

I reached for Wayne's zipper as David and Don began fondling each other's crotches. Then Wayne unbuckled my belt as well. We were all returned missionaries in the same ward in Denver. There were a couple other single men in our congregation, but they didn't hold temple recommends, so we decided not to let them be a part of our group. We existed solely to help each other stay pure enough to marry in the temple as soon as we found the right girl.

Like that was ever going to happen for me.

As Wayne began stroking me, I thought back to the first meeting we had right after the April General Conference. Don had looked around his living room and told us what he'd planned.

"I don't know about you guys," he said, "but I'm having a real hard time not reaching for Carol's boobs every time we go out."

David nodded. "I 'accidentally' brushed up against Samantha's breasts when helping her fasten her seat belt last week."

Don smacked his hands together. "That's just what I mean. If we're not careful, we're not going to be worthy to marry in the temple." He paused for a moment. "But I have a solution."

Don proposed that we meet once a week and give each other hand jobs or blow jobs to release our sexual tension so we wouldn't be as tempted while out with our girlfriends. "It would be a sin if we were gay," he said, "but since we'll mostly be disgusted by it, it's okay. It's just to help us feel less temptation later."

"But doesn't that essentially make it masturbation?" I asked. "Masturbation is a sin."

"True," Don admitted, "but it's the most minor of sexual sins, and we're doing it to make sure we don't commit more grievous sins that also bring down our girlfriends, so it's a good thing."

I thought about Martha Stewart.

"I don't know," David said.

"David," Don asked, "do you want to suck my dick?"

"No."

"Then you're performing a *service*, not a sin. It's like washing the feet of the disciples. It's a sacrifice. We'll get blessings."

I was already on board as soon as Don mentioned his dick, but I wasn't going to be the first to sign up. I knew that since I wasn't straight, it would in fact be a sin for me to participate, but I also thought maybe joining such a group would keep me from leaving the Church to find men on my own. It would be helping me commit lesser sins, too.

My reflections faded away as I began to concentrate more on what Wayne was doing to me tonight. He wasn't the cutest guy in the group, but he gave the best blow jobs. He always went first, though, because he couldn't bear to take anyone else's dick in his mouth after he came.

That wasn't a problem for me.

"Thanks, buddy," I said after I shot. He reached over to kiss me, giving me back all my cum. He didn't like swallowing, but it was so messy spitting out cum onto a hand towel. It was just easier to give it back to me, and I found it helped keep me in the mood longer in any event. I kneeled down and leaned forward into his crotch.

"Oh, Kirstie," he moaned as I began to lick the sides of his penis.

It seemed to me that if he were fantasizing about his girlfriend, then really this sex might still be a sin for him. But I was hardly in a position to judge, so I kept working. Soon, he'd given me his load, and the other two members of our group finished just a moment later. We zipped up, and Don called on David to offer the closing prayer.

If we prayed both before and after, then what we were doing couldn't be a sin.

The meeting adjourned not ten minutes after we'd begun. Drawing out the act any longer would prove we were enjoying ourselves, which would defeat the purpose. We all shook hands and left Don in his apartment to work on his Sunday School lesson. I climbed back into my car and headed home.

When I was a teenager, my bishop had encouraged me to join the Sons of Helaman in order to overcome my masturbation addiction. I'd resisted because masturbation was so often the first step on the road to homosexuality, and I didn't want anyone to become any more suspicious than they might already be. Instead, I had bi-weekly meetings with the bishop to report on my progress. When I turned eighteen, I lied and said my problem was completely under control, and he okayed me for missionary service.

In Denmark, I only masturbated after my companions were asleep. I stood beside their bed two or three times a week while I stroked myself, looking down at them under the covers.

Until Elder Priest woke up while I was in the middle of the act. He promised not to report me if I agreed to let him kiss a teenage girl who lived next door without saying anything to the zone leaders.

Friday morning, I went to my job at Lowe's. I mostly manned the cash register but occasionally had to help out on the floor. I knew almost nothing about construction but enjoyed watching all the men come looking for materials and tools. Today, a guy in his thirties winked at me as I rang up his sale.

I thought about asking if he wanted to have the missionaries come over. But then I decided he might try to seduce them. "You have a good day," I said as I handed him his receipt.

"It'll be better now," he replied, letting his fingers touch mine for a second as he took the paper.

Next Thursday seemed a long time away.

On Sunday, our assigned high councilman visited our ward and addressed the congregation. "I noticed on Facebook and other social media sites that some of you aren't dressing appropriately during the week. You're posting pictures with your shoulders showing or your clothes too tight or wearing leggings and all sorts of other things." Was he talking only to the women, I wondered? "You aren't wearing your garments properly. The thing to remember is that you've made covenants in the temple, and you are to adjust your clothing to accommodate your garments, not the other way around."

In Elders Quorum, Brother Kristofferson kept talking about the "holy Sabbath" and the "holy scriptures." It was all I could do not to shout out "Batman!" every time he used one of those phrases.

I wasn't sure that even our support group meetings would be enough to save my soul. I caught Wayne looking over at me and grinning and wondered if he was feeling weak, too.

Monday night was Single Adult Family Home Evening. Don, Wayne, David, and I were there, of course, but so were most of the other singles from our ward. Carol had to nudge Don so he'd stop looking at her breasts in front of everyone.

David sat so close to Samantha on the sofa that their behavior almost qualified as public petting. Wayne looked at them enviously, Kirstie sitting on the other side of the room, and I just tried to pay attention to the lesson. It was on the importance of serving with the right attitude.

The next day at Lowe's, the cute thirty-something came back to pick up another item. "You'll have to come see my deck after it's finished," he said with a smile.

"Sure," I said. "Sounds fun." The man's smile grew wider and he nodded as he left.

What was wrong with me?

Thursday night seemed so far, far away.

Wayne apparently thought so, too. He called me Tuesday night. "Bryce," he said, "I think I need a special session. You mind if I come over for a few minutes?"

"Anything I can do to help."

When Wayne arrived, he immediately gave me a hug. It went on a little longer than felt natural, but when I tried to pull away, he said, "No, I need more than just someone touching my cock." We continued to hug for another few moments. Then I led him to the sofa.

He shook his head. "Since it's just the two of us, we may as well use the bed. It'll be more comfortable."

I frowned but led him to the bedroom. Once there, Wayne suggested we take off all our clothes this time and not just unzip. Something was definitely up. I hadn't ever suspected Wayne might be gay, but now the possibility seemed more and more likely.

And if we were both gay, then what we were doing would undoubtedly be a sin.

Wayne lay on top of me and began kissing me passionately, sliding his penis between my legs and thrusting gently as he kissed.

Maybe I'd tell him *later* that what we were doing was wrong.

Sex tonight lasted longer than ten minutes. In fact, it lasted longer than thirty. It lasted a full forty-one. Sitting on the edge of the bed, Wayne smiled happily as we dressed, looking over at me a couple of times and giggling. "You want to do that every Tuesday night?" he asked.

"I want you inside me next time," I said.

Wayne stopped buttoning his shirt and stared. "What?"

I shrugged. "We may as well face the facts," I said.

"What facts?" He still wasn't moving.

"That we're gay," I said, my brows furrowing. "Maybe if we—"

"I'm not gay!" Wayne hissed, jumping to his feet.

"I just thought…I thought…"

Wayne looked down at me with an expression of utter disgust. "I'm going to have to tell the others," he said. "You won't be welcome with the Pro-Anti-Nephi-Lehies any longer."

"But…"

"I'll have to tell the bishop, too. You'll probably be excommunicated for having sex."

"Well, *you* just had sex, didn't you?" I pointed out.

"I masturbated," he said. "*You* had sex." He leaned down to put on his shoes while I tried to think of something to say. Then he stormed out of the bedroom and slammed the front door on his way out.

I sat on my bed for a long moment, thinking about what my family was going to think. I wanted to crawl under a rock and die. Provoke a crazy fundamentalist Christian to kill me. Join the Army and fight ISIS.

I'd known all along that for me the support group was a sin, but I couldn't help thinking how much I'd miss seeing Don and David—and Wayne—naked every week. Maybe there was something the bishop could do for me. Something the stake president could do.

Was there a way I could suck them off in their offices as penance? Neither man was very attractive, after all. It wouldn't be like I was enjoying it.

I didn't get much sleep that night and walked into work the next day dragging. All the men at my register seemed particularly unpleasant today. What had I ever seen in guys?

And then he showed up in my line again with a smile.

When I handed him his receipt, I included a slip of paper with my phone number, too.

The Washing Away of Sins

"Elder Andrews!" I heard a voice shouting from somewhere behind me. "Is that really you?"

I turned to see a man in his early forties, a little heavier than I was, a little grayer, carrying a laptop and a small overnight bag. "Elder Guthrie?" I returned. "Oh my God. It's been ages!" I put on my pretend smile.

I'd thrown away all my pictures not only of him but of the other elders I'd worked with as well.

My old mission companion frowned, and I realized I'd slipped in an inappropriate OMG. I reached out my hand and gave him an enthusiastic handshake, a little too strong, in the hopes of redirecting his thoughts. He smiled again and clapped me on the back. "What are you doing here in Phoenix?"

"Layover," I said. "I'm on my way to a medical conference in San Francisco."

"San Francisco?" He frowned again. "There are perverts there."

I laughed, though the comment should have made me angry. Part of me had forgotten how homophobic most Mormons were. It was the reason it had taken me so long to accept my affectional orientation, delaying my coming out until after medical school. But I'd long since stopped caring whether Mormons liked me. "And how about you?" I asked.

"I'm on my way to Mexico City for work. I'll be there a whole week."

"Sounds *excitante*." I spent two months of every year in Central America doing volunteer work with sick children. Those kids often had problems I never saw in my regular practice in Houston.

"Yes, the temple there is lovely," Ethan said. "My wife and I have been to twenty-four different temples, including Mexico City. But I go even when I make a trip without her. Keeps me focused on Judgment Day." He smiled. "So how have you been? Catch me up."

We made our way over to a couple of empty chairs in the waiting area for a flight to Los Angeles and sat down. I set my carry-on at my feet, and Ethan put his bags on the seat next to him. I'd recently broken up with my partner of eight years, but I thought it best not to mention that.

I'd also recently tested positive for HIV after bringing home a guy I met in the park. He'd slipped some sort of date rape drug into my tea and had his way with me after I passed out, clearly without a condom.

Payback?

"Just busy working," I said. "I'm a pediatric physician." There were two presentations I was especially looking forward to over the next couple of days.

Ethan laughed. "Oh, Kent, I always knew you were smart."

"Yeah, well, not too smart. I just got divorced." I clenched my teeth. Why in the world did I blurt that out? Was I going to tell him I'd been excommunicated, too?

"Oh, man, I'm sorry to hear that. Temple divorce?"

"We're definitely not going to be together for eternity."

"Bummer."

"Maybe I'll meet a nice guy in San Francisco." I smiled.

Ethan's mouth fell open. "Don't even joke about something like that."

I nodded. "How about you?" I asked. "What have you been up to?"

Ethan laughed, my inappropriate humor already forgotten. "Let me tell you the latest about Peggy." He laughed again, pulling out his phone to show me some pictures. "She's nine."

Nine, I thought. I closed my eyes, seeing *his*. Then I smiled brightly and motioned for my old companion to go on.

"Peggy didn't have any clean clothes—she's such a tomboy—so she grabbed something out of the dryer to put on before school. When she came home, she said she kept getting the stink eye from her teachers. We live in Sandy, you know. Turns out she'd been wearing the top half of my garments." He chuckled.

"A tomboy," I said.

"Oh, don't worry about that. We'll straighten her out by the time she's a Beehive."

I nodded. Javier had never made it to the age of twelve. Ethan continued talking about his family for the next fifteen or twenty minutes, showing me photo after photo. I still had another hour before I had to turn up at my gate, but I was thinking about lying and telling him my departure time was in half an hour. Eventually, he stopped talking about his wife and kids and began talking about events from our mission.

The last thing I wanted to think about.

"Remember the time Sister Pruitt got caught reading a newspaper?" Ethan asked, chuckling. "Remember the time Elder Simpson beat up his companion for coming on to him?"

"Good times." I didn't think he caught the sarcasm.

Ethan went on for the next few minutes talking about other incidents from our mission days, quirky elders, local sights, mistakes we made with the language.

"Remember that time Sister Crandall broke into our apartment?" Ethan laughed. "She wrote 'Thanks for a fun evening' in lipstick on our bathroom mirror and left her bra on the floor."

"I remember," I said.

"The zone leaders came over and were waiting for us when we got home. Said they'd come to do a surprise apartment inspection. They were so mad. Of course, Sister Crandall had known they were coming, which is why she broke in. Remember how Elder Burton kept waving the bra around?"

I nodded politely. There was no way to casually glance at my watch, but there was a clock on the wall I could see if I turned my head just slightly.

"Elder Creighton kept threatening to call the mission president and have us sent home. Boy, I never felt worse in my life. Can you imagine the disgrace?" He shook his head. "And then of course we eventually find out the whole thing was staged just to torment us."

"And Sister Crandall ended up marrying Elder Burton three months after they both returned home."

Ethan laughed. "Makes you wonder if they pulled that stunt just so he could get his hands on her bra. He did take it with him, if I remember correctly, as 'evidence.'"

"Makes you wonder," I said.

"Man, I think about my mission almost every day. Even all these years later." Ethan smiled and looked down at his laptop in the seat next to his, deep in thought. Would it be okay, I wondered, if I took the lull in conversation as an opportunity to escape? I started to reach down for my bag.

"How about you?" asked Ethan. "Do you think about the mission much?"

If only such a thing were optional. "Javier's baptism," I replied. Now why had I said that?

"Oh."

"Perhaps I should head to my gate," I said.

"It wasn't your fault, Elder Andrews," he said. "I mean, Kent."

Of course it was my fault. "I didn't have to listen to Elder Burton, did I?"

"He was the *zone leader*," Ethan reminded me.

"I shouldn't have listened to him," I said, shaking my head. "I shouldn't have." I closed my eyes, still hearing Elder Burton's voice as he commanded me to immerse Javier into the water again and again and again. The boy was terrified and kept resisting, so he never went completely under. But we could hardly baptize the rest of his family and leave him still unclean.

I wanted to get to the conference, learn something new to help save lives. I wanted to pretend I was a good, noble person.

"You couldn't have known," Ethan said softly. "Who'd ever heard of dry drowning before?"

"It wasn't dry drowning," I said. "It was secondary drowning." Six hours after the family had returned home.

Elder Guthrie shrugged. "He died sinless and went straight to the Celestial Kingdom," he said. "His parents were inactive by the time we finished our missions. He'd have been raised by apostates. You saved that boy's soul."

I spent every day trying to save the lives of young children. But I'd discovered that saving lives didn't redeem me in the least. Those lives *should* have been saved. And the fact that I was doing it proved they *could* be saved. So saving them was the least I could do. I should have been doing that even if I hadn't killed Javier.

As awful as it was to realize, nothing I could do would ever atone for that terrible, stupid mistake. I realized it day after day after day.

Benjamin had grown tired of spending so much time alone each year while I volunteered in Central America.

"I've got to go," I said. "I don't want to miss my flight."

"Elder Andrews…"

I stood up. "It was great to see you again," I said. "I'm glad you have such a nice family." I picked up my bag.

Ethan rose to his feet, too, and wrapped his arms around me tightly. "I'm so sorry," he whispered. "I was the senior. I should have stood up for you. Told the ZLs the baptism was good enough. I'm so sorry."

My heart felt crushed by Ethan's embrace, but I'd cried enough over the years already to refill that baptismal font three times over.

"Pray for me when you're in the temple," I said.

"I will, Elder."

"And let Peggy go on being a tomboy if she wants."

Ethan didn't say anything. I understood. I kissed him on the cheek, gave him one last nod, and walked on to my gate.

Peppercorns at the Preppercon

I opened the door to the convention center in downtown Boise and ushered Brenda and Sean inside. "Don't push me, Doug," said Brenda. "I'm going. I'm going."

"I can't wait to see the guns, Dad," Sean said. "And the bear traps. And body armor."

"We're going to survive the Last Days," I promised. "We're going to be alive when the Savior returns."

"I don't see what's so bad about dying before the Second Coming," Brenda muttered, "and just being resurrected at the start of the Millennium like any normal person."

"The point," I said slowly and for the twentieth time, "is that if we're still alive when the Millennium starts, when we finally do die, we'll pass into our perfected, resurrected state in the twinkling of an eye. That's got to be better than even the best way of dying."

Brenda turned back to give me a look but didn't say anything. She didn't need to. She'd already made it clear that surviving nuclear war and pandemics and societal collapse sounded like a fate worse than death. "I'd rather just be murdered and be done with it," she'd told me more than once. I'd pointed out that it wasn't fair of her to make that same decision for our kids.

We entered the main floor of the convention center and stopped to take everything in. It was our first Preppercon, and the view was breathtaking. Booths selling food and survival equipment and weapons, as far as the eye could see. And hundreds of doomsday preppers, all there with the same goal—to protect their families.

No other success compensated for failure in the home, the family constituting the most important unit of society. Both in this life and the next.

"We were preppers in the Pre-Existence," I said.

"How could you possibly know that, Doug?"

I shrugged. "We were chosen to come to the Earth in the Last Days. That means we were the best fighters in the War in Heaven." Knowing I'd been valiant then was sometimes the only thing which kept me valiant now.

I pointed Brenda and Sean to the far left of the room, and we began walking toward the first row of displayed wares. I wanted to see everything. I was new to prepping, though I'd been Mormon all my life. My parents had tried to maintain a one-year supply of food and other items but had never been all that committed, storing a dozen or so cans of wheat covered with dust in the basement.

Brenda and I had limped along most of our marriage with only a few months of canned goods to help us get through the disasters of the End Times. But then I'd met Dan in the Home Depot restroom, and my world had changed overnight.

"Look at this." Sean stared excitedly at a solar generator.

"That would've come in handy last winter when our power was off for three days," I pointed out.

"There was a blizzard," Brenda replied. "How much sunlight would it have gotten?"

Brenda's attitude had grown harder to bear after I'd spent an hour with Dan at his home in early March. Part of me was still irritated with myself for the infraction. I'd made it to the age of thirty-nine without ever having sex with a man. I'd served a mission, married in the temple, and did my part in providing bodies for four spirits awaiting their turn on Earth.

I'd known all my life about the commandment to have a year's supply, or better yet, a two year's supply, but in the back of my mind, I always thought I'd prefer death so I could have my mortal test over with.

After my time with Dan, dying from something I could prevent sounded like suicide.

Not that I could prevent the apocalypse, of course. But I could prevent being unprepared for it.

"Here's a gas-powered generator, too," said Sean. He was my eldest at fifteen and the only one of the children who wanted to come to the convention today. "Who would want that when you can get a solar one?"

I shrugged. "Maybe it has more power and can be used for isolated important tasks."

"Can it split the heavens open and make Jesus come back?" Brenda asked.

"Now, honey."

We passed a booth selling cans of diethylene glycol for cooking. Next to that were a solar cooker and a solar water purifier. Plus a sample five gallon water storage container and, finally, the natural outcome of all these things, a latrine kit and sanitation packs.

"I don't want to go potty in an outhouse." Brenda shook her head. "Can't we just die? I'm sure there's plumbing in Paradise.

"If we neglect our duty to our kids," I said, "we'll end up in Spirit Prison."

"And Spirit Prison doesn't have plumbing?"

Sean laughed. "You guys crack me up. We won't have bodies after we die. Not until the resurrection. There's no reason for either Paradise *or* Spirit Prison to have plumbing."

"Don't you think Jesus ever visits the prisoners?" Brenda asked. "Or Peter, James, and John? Or other people who've already been resurrected?"

"Oh, Mom. Jesus doesn't need to sit on a toilet. You are so gross."

"One thinks about these things when one is always the person who ends up cleaning the bathroom." She paused. "Because certain kids refuse to do their chores."

"Stop bickering, you two," I said. "We're here to get some ideas for our year's supply." I nudged them and they continued on. The truth was I still didn't know if I wanted to survive, if Dan wasn't going to be there with me. The way he touched me was magical. Though I supposed it was probably dark magic. I'd broken things off after that first morning, but I knew I was still damned. I couldn't risk telling the bishop and having the stake president convene a court. My soul was lost.

But that fact made it all the more important for me to make sure my family was provided for. If I could just make sure Brenda and the kids made it to the Celestial Kingdom, it didn't matter if I was exiled to Outer Darkness. And while letting them die sooner would mean their tests were over, too, I couldn't let their deaths be on their own heads, either. They knew about the commandment as much as I did. We had to be prepared.

Brenda, Sean, and I meandered down the first aisle and into the second and then the third. I'd never known how much there was to prepping. There was fishing tackle. There were first aid supplies, DVDs to help people train for hand-to-hand combat, to train for hunting, to train for construction, for skinning a deer, for detecting poisonous plants, for treating people who had been poisoned.

Apparently, people were supposed to watch and memorize all these *before* the electricity went out, though it was possible, I supposed, that a DVD player could be hooked up to one of the solar generators. We stopped and read the information provided at each of the booths, as if we were reading the placards in a museum.

I wondered if I'd be raped by roving gangs, and if that would be a good thing or not. Part of me thought maybe it would be better if Brenda was killed by whatever disaster was coming. She clearly didn't want the misery of post-apocalyptic living, and if she died before the collapse, maybe Heavenly Father would be more understanding if I ended up with a man. I'd *need* a man to help me survive, and surviving was good, wasn't it?

I wondered what it would be like, though, if my entire family was wiped out. Then it wouldn't really matter if I sinned or not. They'd all have safely finished their tests. They'd all be bound for the Celestial Kingdom. It didn't matter if I failed. The important thing was that they'd all be saved.

"I am not living on tomato powder." Brenda pointed to a display. "Or onion powder or egg powder or peanut butter powder."

"They can all be reconstituted," I said. I looked at the other foods available. There was instant mashed potatoes, steel cut oats, and a whole variety of freeze dried foods—chicken cubes, strawberries, banana chips, peaches, apples, green beans, broccoli, asparagus—the list went on and on. "Look, sweetheart," I said. "They have dried honey powder. It's not like we won't have *any* luxuries."

Not only was there powdered milk but one could also buy powdered chocolate milk, for fussy survivors, I supposed. There was food with a twenty-five-year guaranteed shelf life.

Who was one going to complain to if one had to follow up on the warranty?

"I want real food," Brenda said. "Can't we just buy canned peaches and canned corn and rotate our food supply?"

"When are we gonna get to the cool stuff?" Sean interrupted. "You said there'd be machetes."

"All in good time," I replied. "All in good time."

Good time. How could it be that thirty-nine years of dedication and sacrifice and work could be erased by the sins of one solitary hour? Was sin that much more powerful than righteousness?

Maybe it was. It took a hundred years of dedication to preserve public parks, which could be ruined in less than a year by logging and drilling. It could take three hundred years, a thousand years, maybe longer, to build up a great city like Aleppo, only to have it wiped out in months by warfare. It was always easier to destroy. The same was clearly true of our salvation as well.

But if I was willing to live in a war-ravaged world, why couldn't I also be willing to live in a war-ravaged soul? If life was worth living after the apocalypse, it was worth living after sin, too.

I looked at the last of the food items on display. Powdered cheese. Peppercorns. Cinnamon. Salt. Paprika. One would certainly need something to spice up the dreary life which awaited us. Thousands of seed packets of different species to restart the entirety of agriculture.

If a post-apocalyptic world could be redeemed by the return of the Savior, why couldn't a post-apocalyptic soul?

There was a difference between surviving and living.

I wished I'd kept Dan's phone number.

I looked at a booth selling matches, condoms, toothbrushes, and other daily necessities in packs of a hundred.

"Gas masks!" said Sean. "Cool!"

The area code had been the same as mine, and the first three numbers. Then there was a 7, a 9, and an 8, but I couldn't remember the order. Or what the fourth number was.

I could hardly hang out in the bathroom for hours hoping to be there if Dan ever came back.

Was there some reason *Brenda* wanted so desperately to die?

What if being with *me* was a fate worse than death?

There were booths with info on how to build a safe house, booths selling tents, booths with contractors advertising their skills.

"Finally!" Sean said. "Knives! And look at that cool archery set!"

"I'm tired," said Brenda. "Can we take a break and go have lunch?" She looked about with her nose wrinkled. "Someplace with real food?"

"Aw, Mom, we're just about to get to the guns."

"Just a little longer, sweetheart," I said.

Brenda sighed and we kept walking. The gun section of the floor was by far the largest part. There seemed no end to the multitude of life-saving weaponry and the various types of ammo one needed for each of them. Some of the vendors allowed Sean to handle the firearms, and he smiled broadly as he aimed at both me and his mother.

If only the gun were loaded, I thought. If only one could go off accidentally.

The idea made me look around the room with new eyes. Wouldn't it be great, I thought, if some nut job came in with the idea of killing the people most likely to be his competition after the apocalypse? He could start shooting up the place. I could go to confront him and die a hero.

Surely, that would make up for Dan.

What would someone have to do, I wondered, to make up for a lifetime of Dans? For a sinful, wonderful relationship that lasted twenty years?

I looked at Brenda. Perhaps what I really needed to do was start making up for a lifetime of Doug.

"Who's up for a burger, fries, and a milk shake?" I asked.

Brenda smiled.

"This'll all be more fun for you on a full stomach, Sean."

He rubbed his chin. I knew he didn't want to leave, but he was never one to pass up a milk shake.

"Then I'll take you home, honey," I said to Brenda, "and Sean and I will finish up here on our own."

Brenda's smile widened. "Just don't buy anything," she said, wagging a finger. I gave her a kiss, and we headed for the exit.

I would let Sean wander around the convention center by himself after we got back, let him enjoy the idea of adventure. I would let him think misery was fun. I would try to convince myself of the same thing.

I would pretend I was interested in life, while I looked about the room for any survivalist at all who looked the least little bit like Dan.

Two Much of a Good Thing

"Gareth, I want you to cut off your dick." Martin looked at me with such a serious expression that I knew this was a deal breaker. If I didn't agree, he wouldn't marry me.

"I—I'll have to think about it," I replied.

Martin's lip curled just a little before he nodded. "If you don't love me more than you love your dick," he said, "this marriage will never work."

I obviously wanted this marriage to work. Martin was good for me. He'd made me stop going to church. He'd forced me to ask my boss for a raise, which I got. He'd required me to "volunteer" at a soup kitchen once a month. He continually pushed me to do all sorts of things for my own good. And I'd never seen a more attractive man.

I didn't have enough experience with black men to know if the stereotypes were true, but his great, massive dick was far more impressive than what I had to offer. "I'd better head home then," I said, "and start thinking." I wanted a home with Martin. We couldn't afford a house yet, even with our combined incomes. But maybe a condo.

Martin said condos were like gay marriage. Not quite the real thing. But he was open to both.

"Don't call me unless you're willing to move ahead with our relationship."

I moved to kiss him goodbye and he pulled back. I didn't force the issue but instead turned around and left Martin's apartment without another word. I sat in my Ford Fusion for several minutes before starting the ignition. What Martin was asking, I told myself, was unreasonable. No normal man would cut off his dick for any reason. The thing could be gangrenous and a normal man wouldn't part with it.

But then, I wasn't normal, was I? Some early cell during my fetal development had divided, but my body hadn't recognized the division. Each of those dedicated cells continued to form a penis of its own. While I only had one prostate and one scrotum, I had two perfectly formed penises.

They both worked, too. My urine stream seemed equally divided, and both penises ejaculated at the same time, even if only one of them was being stimulated. I'd fantasized about sex with men for years before my timid Mormon soul found the courage to come out, but in all my dreams, other gay men were *happy* to discover my irregularity. The truth, unfortunately, was that most of them were completely turned off.

"You're a freak," the first guy I ever went to bed with told me before kicking me out of his apartment.

"Maybe you're the Devil," said a young Southern Baptist I brought to my own place.

One guy worried that I might be radioactive. Another that I might be contagious, that he might start sprouting extra penises all over his body like warts if he touched me.

"You're too much to handle," another guy explained. "I've never been able to take two dicks up my ass at the same time."

"I can fuck you with just one," I pointed out. "The other will just rub up against you on the outside."

He shook his head, and I began to wonder if I would forever remain a virgin. But then I'd met Martin. At first, he was intrigued, enough to suck me off, anyway, though he did jump in surprise when one load hit him in the cheek just as I was cumming in his mouth. We'd continued dating off and on, and though he never seemed to love my second dick, I thought he loved *me* and so had proposed to him tonight.

When I arrived back at my apartment, I went to my bedroom, laid my cum towel on the bed, and beat off. The left dick always shot just a tiny bit farther than the right.

Would someone ever ask another person to cut off an arm? Or an ear?

Or a second testicle, for that matter?

I was twenty-five years old. I didn't want to face a lifetime alone. And with all the stress I felt these days, I needed a meaningful change in my life. Either a new job, a move to another city, a return to church. Or marriage.

Martin always had me lie face down when we had sex so he couldn't see my dicks as he fucked me from behind. I could live with that. Especially since I could never get enough of what he had to offer.

Martin wanted me to ask for a promotion at work, in addition to the raise I already received. I could live with that, too, if I had to stay with the company.

I didn't know why the fact that I had two dicks was so overwhelming to people. I didn't understand why even having just one dick should be such a big deal. There was more to a relationship than sex. Or a perfect body.

I closed my eyes and could see Martin as clearly as if he were standing in the room.

I slept fitfully during the night and woke up early Sunday morning. Looking at the clock, I wondered if I should go to services for a change. It would make Mom happy, and that was worth a little effort. And I missed the little spiritual lessons I used to hear. Martin had me read the entire Harry Potter series to reset my moral compass. It was certainly more readable than the Book of Mormon, but I missed singing "Count Your Blessings." I showered, put on my gray suit, and jumped in the car.

"Look what the cat dragged in," Mom said when I approached her in the foyer.

"It's good to see you, son," said my dad, giving me a hug.

"Hi, Gareth," said my sister. Tina had just returned from a mission to South Africa, which seemed to be a completely different experience than what I'd had in Brazil. She'd come home more prejudiced against blacks than when she left, and that was saying something.

"Are you here to confess to the bishop?" Mom asked.

"Is there something he doesn't already know?" I returned.

Dad put his arm around my shoulders, and we headed to priesthood opening exercises while Mom and Tina started off for the Relief Society room. Dad was a high priest, though, so soon he marched off to the high council room while I stayed in the chapel with the other elders. My old Single Adult friends Jay and Stanley were there. They never called anymore after I came out, but they seemed friendly enough today. Stanley flashed me a picture of his girlfriend on his phone. Gabrielle from the Norcross ward, far, but still part of our Atlanta stake.

The lesson focused on the Doctrine and Covenants, in particular the passage which said that the Second Coming might happen by the time Joseph Smith turned eighty-five. At one point during the lesson, the topic diverged into signs of the times, and Brother Behrens talked about all the promiscuity on television, and the lack of chastity in women's clothing in general.

"Heavenly Father sent AIDS to cleanse the Earth of gays," Jay added to the thread on immorality. "Satan fought back and helped doctors develop a treatment." He didn't look at me as he said it. "But Heavenly Father is smarter than Satan. He'll send another plague on the gays before long."

The topic then shifted to other calamities of the Last Days—wars and tornadoes and droughts and earthquakes.

I didn't stay for Sunday School or Sacrament meeting.

But I got a call a couple of hours later. "Hi, son," my dad said. "Your mother enjoyed seeing you at church today. She wants to know if you'll come over for lunch."

Mom never placed a call to me herself. When Tina and I were children, she would take my sister to the public swimming pool, while I would have to stay home and find something to do on my own. I usually read a book, which always gave unconditional love. Tina often pointed out that Mom breast fed her but bottle fed me, something neither of us could remember without Mom's constant repetition of the fact. She'd been suspicious of my sexuality years before she knew I was gay.

With two penises, she said, she knew there'd be trouble of *some* kind. "Too much man is a bad thing," she always told me. I, on the other hand, thought I could never get enough man.

My dad had handled things differently. He knew I was afraid to take gym class in junior high and high school, that I didn't want to change clothes in front of the other boys. Dad suggested I take band class instead. As it turned out, though, choosing the flute didn't help me escape regular bouts of rough teasing. But at least my secret was safe.

Guys whose sole secret was their sexual orientation didn't know how good they had it.

I wondered if I could ask Dad about my predicament with Martin. There were so few other people I could talk to these days. My friend Ryan sometimes, though that was uncomfortable because he wanted to be more than friends. My friend Brett, but his straightness prevented him from fully understanding the gay world.

Dad had never been freaked out by my second dick the way Mom was. He even joked once about my own personal Second Cumming.

"Sure, Dad, be right over. Thanks."

Tina helped Mom fry up some chicken while Dad and I were banished to the living room. We talked Falcons for a bit, about our abnormally hot weather, and about a recent terrorist attack in Madrid. Then I blurted out what Martin had said. Dad stopped talking and looked at the floor a long moment.

"I do wish you'd marry a young woman," he said finally, "or at least donate at a fertility clinic." He sighed. "You might not be a one-time accident, you know. You might be able to pass on your gift through your genes."

"My gift?"

Dad nodded. "It's a gift, Gareth. If Martin doesn't see that…"

Tina came in the living room a moment later with a look on her face which suggested she might have been eavesdropping. "Lunch is ready."

Dad offered a blessing on the food, and I scooped some fried yellow squash onto my plate. Tina talked about a woman she'd taught in Johannesburg, Mom talked about the Davises' new baby, and Dad talked about a problem at the plant. No one asked anything about me, and I decided not to volunteer any more than I'd told Dad before we began eating.

Mom casually mentioned a young woman, "pretty," who'd just moved into the ward, and when I didn't take the bait, she mentioned a class the ward was conducting for young couples on their way to the temple. I didn't take that bait, either. So just as the meal was coming to an end, Mom decided on a more direct approach. "Gareth," she said, "you meet any nice young women at work lately?"

Did Mom honestly believe women would react to my deformity better than gay men? That they'd react any better than *she* had?

"Yes," I said, watching Mom's eyes light up, which I somehow found irritating. "Lily's great. She's smart and funny and just a year younger than I am." And about the only nice person in my department. I had to make a change soon.

"You going to ask her out?" Mom continued, trying to sound casual.

"Oh, I don't think her husband would like that," I said. I remembered that Lily said Clark's workplace was looking for new people.

Dad laughed and Mom's jaw tightened. "The problem with telling gays they're going to hell," she said icily, "is that gays are so faithless they can't imagine hell being real. Outer Darkness is too abstract for people who can't feel the Spirit. We need to do something more concrete for them."

"Concrete?" asked Tina. I wasn't about to encourage the conversation.

"The government should confiscate the property of gays," Mom went on. "Revoke their licenses. Invalidate their degrees. Then they'd see the light and repent. No one wants to lose their money. You just need to give gays the proper incentive."

I wondered if I should admit I was thinking of taking a lower paying job, pretty much anywhere, just to escape the unhappiness I felt at work.

Tina laughed. "We had a gay elder in my mission. The mission president sent him home."

"The least your father and I should do," Mom said, waving her fork at me, "is write you out of our will. But your dad won't have it." She shook her head. "We realize that inheriting our money seems so far in the future that doesn't feel real, either."

"I think it's a great idea," Tina said.

"Is there any dessert?" Dad asked. Mom gave him a cold stare.

"I proposed to Martin last night," I said. Martin didn't like to read, I remembered. Not even articles on the vast number of sexual irregularities among humans. Androgen Insensitivity Syndrome alone was fascinating. And that was just the tip of Laban's sword.

I hated that I still thought like a Mormon.

The conversation stopped dead for a moment. Finally, Mom cleared her throat. "Gays should be castrated." She set her fork down and then stood up and began collecting plates. "Not physically, of course, just chemically. That way it's reversible if they repent."

"How thoughtful."

"They should be given a year or two of probation to change their ways, and if they don't change, *then* we should physically castrate them. We can't waste our whole lives with people who won't help themselves."

Martin refused to introduce me to his parents. He refused to meet mine as well. There was a reason, I thought, that two people were supposed to leave their parents and cleave to each other.

I wanted to ask Mom how she intended to deal with lesbians. Female circumcision? But I didn't really want to pursue this train of thought any longer than necessary.

"Martin wants to get married right away," I lied.

Mom threw a glass into the sink, where it shattered. "What we need is a Holocaust for homos," she said, her hands trembling.

"But that still places the burden on us." She pointed her index finger at me, jabbing it as she spoke. "You should just kill yourself now and make the world a better place."

Even for Mom, this was extreme. It was as if she thought my marrying Martin somehow invalidated her marriage to Dad. But her cruelty didn't pierce me the way Martin's request had. I didn't expect *her* to be my soulmate.

Was asking me to have surgery to become normal really such a terrible thing?

I watched as Mom turned to the sink and began gathering up the broken glass.

"Gareth," Tina said, "you bring destruction everywhere you go."

I stood up. Dad was looking down at his plate, unwilling to say anything, which made my throat constrict. I wondered if too much religion was good for anyone, even a person who fit into religious norms. I kissed him on the top of his head. "Thanks for lunch, Mom," I said. Then I walked out of the house.

But I couldn't go home, though I wasn't sure exactly why. I should call Martin, I told myself, and agree to any conditions he had. He was clearly so much healthier for me than my family. And I'd long ago realized that no one was perfect. I drove around aimlessly for forty-five minutes, finally stopping in front of Ryan's condo.

He was older than Martin, almost fifty, the color of latte, and the only other man who'd ever agreed to have sex with me. But I had a whole life to look forward to. I wasn't ready to begin dealing with the problems of aging at my age.

Though, to be fair, Ryan wasn't decrepit, had been able to cum twice both times we had sex. That was better than my once divided by two. It was too bad his penis was no larger than either of mine.

Why did everything have to be about sex?

"What a pleasant surprise," Ryan said as he opened the door. He pulled me in and gave me a hug. "To what do I owe the pleasure?"

I wanted to ask him what he thought of Martin's ultimatum, but after we settled into the sofa, I told him about today's lunch instead. He suggested I only talk to my father in the future, never my mother, and away from my parents' house. I wondered why Martin had never forced me to make that change. I nodded at Ryan and asked him how he'd been.

"Gone to a couple of plays with this one guy," he said, "but I don't think anything's going to come of it. The plays were comedies, and he didn't laugh."

Martin never liked going to the theatre. "I'm sorry." But he did like binge watching *Scorpion* and *Lucifer* and other shows. That was always fun.

"Let me ask you something." Ryan picked up his remote and pulled up Roku and then YouTube. "What do you think of this?" I was debating how to bring the conversation around to Martin's counterproposal to my proposal when he clicked and a clip showing two black men confronted by zombies appeared on the screen.

As the men start to run, they notice that the zombies nearest them flinch as they pass. One of the men looks confused and then notices a zombie in a car quickly locking the door when she sees the two men. The black man looks thoroughly disgusted and turns to his friend. "Mother-fuckin' racist zombies!" he rants.

I laughed.

Ryan smiled.

Then he looked at my crotch. I used to be embarrassed I had such a nice package. Then I was grateful. And lately I was starting to feel embarrassed again. "You want to come into the bedroom for a while?"

"Martin wants me to cut off one of my dicks."

Ryan stared at me in shock for a moment, and then his eyebrows furrowed. "Tell him to go fuck himself," he said. "With his own dick." He smiled. "It might require him to get a knife for himself."

It was exactly what I wanted to hear, but now that I heard it, I wasn't sure it was very helpful. I *loved* Martin. He'd helped me to finally stop praying. He'd made me stop wearing garments. He'd introduced me to alcohol.

It seemed ungrateful not to be…grateful.

"At the very least," Ryan continued, "don't agree to anything just yet. Date him another six months first."

"But I *want* to be married," I said. "I'm so tired of being alone." I could hear the neediness in my voice and felt disgust. I almost felt too comfortable with that emotion. Even Dad's love couldn't make up for a lifetime of Mom's disgust.

"You don't think you'll feel alone with someone who doesn't accept you for who you are?"

I didn't say anything.

"Look, Gareth," Ryan said, "husbands are like condos." He spread his arms to indicate his. "Even if you've fully paid for the condo, there are still dues and special assessments, so you end up paying what amounts to a full mortgage payment every month for something you thought was already yours. There's a price to pay for every relationship." He looked down at the floor and then back up at me again. "That's true not just of partners," he said. "Friends cost continual maintenance, too."

So was he telling me the cost of being Martin's husband was just a normal expense?

Who wanted to be normal?

When Martin insisted I stop fasting the first Sunday of each month, he said, "I'll always look out for you, Gareth."

Was there a point at which support became control?

I looked again at Ryan. The only thing he'd ever ordered me to do was bend over.

I wished I could cum twice. Or four times. Or however the math worked out.

Ryan could apparently read my expression because he stood and held out his hand. Would it be such a terrible thing to date him again for a few months? It wasn't as if he was going to be too old in the immediate future. I almost laughed, thinking that if I did break up with Martin, I wouldn't even have to tell him to his face. He'd already said not to call him unless I was willing to undergo surgery, taking the hardest part of breaking up out of my hands.

I took Ryan's hand and followed him to the bedroom. But the sex didn't go very well. Ryan couldn't even get hard. "I'm too intimidated," he said. "Let's just watch a DVD while I hold you." He slipped in some porn and we cuddled in bed. I wondered if this would be enough if it was all I had on a regular basis.

I could almost feel Martin's big cock inside me. The thought made both of my own twitch. The movie was routine at first, but then a black man came on who had a dick at least fifteen inches long. No wider than a normal dick, so the thing looked bizarre. And not terribly appealing. To me.

I sat up straight.

"What is it?"

"Do you think anyone would hire me to do a movie?" I asked.

"Are you kidding?" Ryan laughed. "Do you know the kind of stuff that's out there?" He shook his head at my lack of insight. "I'd watch it."

If I made a few films, I thought, I might get fan mail. I could take my time and find someone who liked the Two Nephites just as they were, someone who'd be happy to add his own Third Nephite to the mix.

It might be better to wait till the pool of possible spousal candidates was larger than two. Mormon men who'd just returned from their missions usually ended up with the first woman they dated for longer than three weeks. There was no reason I shouldn't date four men before making a commitment. Or ten. Or fifteen. Could I ever have too much of a good thing?

In some movie the other night that I'd watched alone after Martin left, one of the characters said something about needing to enjoy your own company if you ever expected to be happy in a relationship.

It was self-evident when it applied to others but never felt true for the person who wasn't content. We wanted someone else to make us happy when we couldn't do it ourselves.

I wasn't ready for a condo assessment yet, that much was clear. Perhaps it was better that I just pay maintenance costs on a few friends for now. I might have enough to do so if I started handling my own resources. Enough for Ryan, anyway. And maybe Brett. Maybe even Lily and her husband. And a fan or two.

I could save up for a house.

"You're getting hard," I said, nodding toward Ryan's member.

"It's that talk of you making movies."

The idea had never occurred to me before, and already it was feeling normal. I wondered if my mom was right about gays being decadent and perverted. But the idea didn't particularly bother me. Of course, maybe that said more about my soul than I cared to admit.

And maybe it didn't.

I straddled Ryan and motioned for him to turn over. "Get on your stomach," I said. "I'm going to fuck you twice." I smiled. "For once."

He nodded with a smile of his own and handed me a bottle of lube. When we finished, we got dressed and went back in the living room. Ryan showed me a copy of *The Mormon Erotica Writer* that he'd bought "to try to understand Mormon sexuality better."

He lay down on the sofa with his head in my lap. "After you read me a couple of chapters," he said, "let's watch some *Key and Peele*." I leaned down and gave him a kiss. Then I opened the book, cleared my throat, and began to read.

Recruiting Gays

"There's a space." Walt pointed. "Park there, Mort."

I squeezed into the tiny space between two cars on North Rampart in the Faubourg Marigny, just south of the French Quarter. I'd always been good at parallel parking. Mom could never hide her envy. Dad was worse at parking than Mom, but he rarely showed his emotions, so I didn't know if he was impressed or instead irritated that I was better at something than he was.

I couldn't wait to graduate school next month and move out of the house. At least these activities with the Single Adults helped me feel grown up.

After I turned off the motor, we all stepped out of the car. The service project had been Walt's idea, but Toby, Connor, and Boyd had come along, too. Cassie, Dawn, and Sally were in a separate car. They were already waiting for us in the parking lot of the Robért Supermarket across the street. "I'm nervous," Sally said. "What if they beat us up?"

Walt laughed. "No one's beating anyone up. If Daniel can go into the lion's den, we can certainly go into a gay bar."

"But how will anyone feel the Spirit in such a depraved atmosphere?" I asked. It had been my biggest concern since Walt suggested the activity. My best friend, Grant, had outright refused to come. He was home watching *Game of Thrones* while I was stuck here trying to convert people who were drinking.

Mom and Dad wouldn't let me watch *Game of Thrones*.

"Even Laman and Lemuel felt the Spirit when Nephi spoke," Walt pointed out.

"That didn't keep them from tying him up and beating him, though, did it?" Sally reminded us.

Walt sighed. "If you want to wait in the car while the rest of us go in to do the Lord's work, feel free." He waved his arm to indicate the general direction of the vehicles. I could see Sally quickly surveying the poor neighborhood, dimly lit and foreboding, with broken glass on the sidewalk and some food containers for Kentucky Fried Chicken a few feet away along the curb. She didn't say anything else.

"Here's Moby Dick on the corner," Walt said. "The guys will go in here. The Lace and Leather is over on the other side of Elysian Fields. You girls go in there." He looked at his watch. "Now remember, we have church tomorrow, so we can't stay too late. One hour and then we meet back here."

"Should we have a prayer first?" asked Dawn.

Walt turned to frown at two young black men passing by. Both displayed large portions of underwear as their pants drooped to the tops of their thighs. "Pray in your hearts," he said. "Let's go."

While the girls headed to the lesbian bar, Walt led the guys to the entrance of the Moby Dick. A muscled, tattooed man sat in a chair on the sidewalk, checking IDs. He looked at us suspiciously but waved us inside. I felt like a soldier going into battle.

My Patriarchal Blessing had said I'd been a general in the War in Heaven, so I didn't know why I felt this scared. I'd always hated knocking on doors on my mission, too. If I was the type of general Heavenly Father promoted, it was amazing we'd won the battle in the first place.

I trembled as I crossed the threshold of the bar. The place was so dark it took a minute for my eyes to adjust. My ears demanded more of my attention, though, because of the pounding music. How were we supposed to talk to anyone over this racket?

"Mort." Walt nudged me. "Go buy a 7-Up."

At least, that's what I thought he said. I walked up to the bar and ordered my drink. Toby, Connor, and Boyd split up and squeezed up to the bar in different places. We were going solo for the next hour. I left an extra dollar on the bar as a tip, though I hated supporting this decadent lifestyle. I just didn't want the bartender saying anything bad about me to the other patrons and jeopardizing our plan.

Walt had explained that he'd come to the French Quarter on Mardi Gras a few weeks earlier and seen two things which affected him deeply. The first was all those gay men flashing their penises for beads. The other was a group of Christians carrying signs demanding repentance and dragging a large wooden cross through the streets.

"I decided that if people following the wrong church could be bold enough to confront gays," Walt told us, "then we could do even better. They weren't interacting with anyone personally. If we approach people one on one, we can win some of these poor souls to our side."

"Why not just infiltrate Notre Dame seminary over on Carrollton?" I asked.

Walt frowned. "That's not a bad idea for another service project," he said.

This didn't really seem like a service project to me. Service was helping clean Rosette's place after it sustained smoke damage from the fire in her neighbor's apartment. It was helping Xiomara move out to Metairie. It was putting together the yard sale to benefit Single Adults too poor to pay for admittance to the Singles Conference in Pensacola. Tonight's effort seemed more like plain old missionary work. I'd gotten enough of that during my two years in Sweden.

I found a spot along the front of the bar nearest Elysian Fields. The wall to my right was covered with posters advertising drag shows and leathermen contests, plus one for an AIDS benefit and another promoting condoms. The wall on the far side of the room sported a couple of Mardi Gras masks, an acrylic painting depicting an unspeakable act, and a whip.

These people were freaks.

I forced myself to turn away from the painting and surveyed my immediate surroundings. A guy about my age, in his mid-twenties, rolled a white ball on the pool table in front of me, making it ricochet over and over again. My uncle had a pool table in his house, "sinful," my mother always said, but then my uncle had left the Church before I was even born, so what could one expect?

I never told Mom that I played the game with my cousins while she sat in the living room talking to her brother. I sometimes played gin rummy with a neighbor boy as well. It was amazing I'd still been worthy when it came time to go on a mission.

I walked up to the guy playing with the cue ball. "Wanna play?" I asked.

"What?" He put his hand to his ear.

"Wanna play?" I shouted.

The man looked me up and down and then nodded. I found a cue stick on the wall behind me while the other guy racked the balls. I hadn't played since before my mission, so I let the gay guy break. Two balls immediately flew into various pockets. "Stripes," he said.

"What's your name?" I shouted.

"Patrick." He didn't ask mine.

"Mort," I shouted.

He nodded.

We played for six or seven minutes. Patrick got all his balls plus the eight before I even got two of mine. "Not bad," I said.

"I like getting things into holes."

He said it with a straight face, but I could feel my own turning warm. "You come here often?" I asked.

"All the time. I live just a few blocks away." I felt a chill, wondering if he was going to try luring me back to his place. I had to do something quickly to be proactive.

"This is my first time," I said. "I'm a little nervous."

"How did you come to choose the Moldy Dick?"

"Excuse me?"

"That's what us regulars call the bar." He laughed.

"Oh, I…I just looked up gay bars, and this one seemed to have more access to parking. So many of the other bars are in the Quarter."

"This is what we call a neighborhood bar," he said. "We like to be neighborly here." He leaned into me and gave me a kiss before I could pull away. My stomach churned, but I was here to save this man's soul. I thought about the fight in the Pre-Existence again. Spirits didn't have blood to spill. I wondered what happened when you sliced a spirit arm off.

Surely a perfect God would have weapons more powerful than swords and spears. Were there spirit machine guns? I felt Patrick trying to force his tongue between my lips and frantically debated what to do. Leading him on was the whole point of the activity, wasn't it? I wished I understood military strategy. I opened my lips and let his tongue in.

I'd never even French kissed a girl before. I tried to slide my tongue into Patrick's mouth as well, hoping I was doing it right. This was the kind of thing soldiers did all the time.

What kind of a war, though, could it have been back up there in heaven? After all, every one of those spirits who'd lost was still alive and well. Some of them were probably here right now, whispering in the ears of these men, egging them on.

Patrick pressed the rest of his body into me. I could feel something hardening in his jeans and broke off the kiss. "Too fast?" he asked with a grin.

"Y-yeah."

"You wanna come over and see my sling?" he went on. Exactly as I thought. These guys only had one thing on their minds. "We can just sleep together tonight. I promise I won't fuck you till tomorrow morning after breakfast."

What in the world had Walt been thinking when proposing this lame idea? Gays were beyond salvaging. Even gay people who'd been in the Church their whole lives could rarely be saved. Just last week, I read a story about a former bishop and stake president who'd been the chief architect for almost forty temples. He'd had a sex change operation, destroying his family, and promptly been excommunicated. How could I ever hope to save someone who'd never even heard of the Book of Mormon before?

"I never date people until I see them in church first," I replied.

Patrick laughed. "Don't go on many dates, do you?"

I went on lots of dates, I wanted to tell him. *Decent* people went to church all the time. I just didn't like Dawn or Sally or Cassie or Rosette that way. I was thinking of applying to grad school at the University of Utah just so I could have a larger pool of faithful women to draw from. "What do you have against church?" I asked.

"How much time do we have?"

I glanced at my watch. About forty-five minutes, but I didn't want to tell him that. Patrick turned his back to me and pressed me against the wall with his behind. He grabbed both my arms and put them around his chest, spending the next few minutes telling me about growing up Catholic.

It was odd talking to the back of someone's head. He explained that he'd gone to confession regularly as a teenager, admitting each time to playing with his "wee-wee." The priest finally yelled at him. "It's a penis!"

From that day on, Patrick decided to face his sexuality as an adult. He started having sex with classmates in high school and then once he turned eighteen with guys he picked up in bars. And at work. And at the store. "Gay guys are everywhere," he said.

"That's what I'm afraid of," I said, not realizing I'd spoken the words aloud.

Why would Heavenly Father make people gay in the first place, I wondered? It didn't make any sense.

Patrick reached behind him and gently squeezed my crotch. "You don't *feel* too afraid," he pointed out.

It was a simple physiological reaction, I wanted to tell him. It didn't mean I was attracted to him.

After several more minutes, Patrick went up to the bar to get another drink. Obviously an alcoholic. "Want anything?" he asked. I shook my head.

While he was gone, I looked about the room to see how the other Singles were faring. Toby and Connor were laughing with a man in a cowboy hat and cowboy boots. Boyd looked like he was about to piss his pants, a man in leather chaps pinching his nipples. Walt was nowhere to be seen.

But I also looked about at the other men scattered throughout the place. Several were standing alone, looking bored. There was a group of four men chatting and sharing photos from their phones. One man was rocking out to the music by himself. And another man ate popcorn at the bar.

One might not even realize at first that all these men were going to hell.

Patrick came back a moment later, took a sip of his drink, and then demanded we change positions, him against the wall with my back up against him. He rubbed my chest with one hand while he continued drinking with the other.

Completely perverted. We should all get up and leave right now. There was no hope of accomplishing anything. In the Pre-Existence, we had *fought* the bad guys, not tried to convert them.

How was it we felt we had won, though, when all we really ended up doing was living in separate places? I'd heard of the gay ghetto before. Was there such a thing as a Celestial ghetto, too?

Patrick nibbled on my ear.

"So," I said, "would you like to come to church with me tomorrow?"

"Aha!" he replied, now kissing my neck. "That means you like me."

"I just…I mean…I…"

Patrick laughed. "Sure, I'll tag along." He took another sip. "Just be prepared to come back to my place afterward."

I could promise anything I had to, I thought. It didn't mean I had to do it. "Okay." I got Patrick's phone number and address and then pulled him close to kiss him on the lips, to clinch the deal. I wondered if my non-alcohol mouthwash would disinfect my lips sufficiently when I got home. "See you tomorrow morning at 9:30."

"Ugh. That early?"

"Church starts at 10:00."

"You better be worth it." He laughed and took another sip of his drink. The smell was nauseating.

I headed out of the bar and crossed the street, joining Cassie and Walt already in the parking lot. "Any luck?" I asked. They both shook their heads. I wondered if Walt had even tried. He looked abnormally pale in the dim street lighting.

Before long, the rest of the group trickled out to join us. Dawn said she got one lesbian to agree to church tomorrow, and Toby said the guy he and Connor talked to had agreed to Single Adult volleyball on Wednesday. When Walt asked how Boyd had done, he just mumbled, "I don't want to talk about it."

"Well, that's two people coming to church tomorrow." Walt began looking more like his old self again. "If we can get them to repent, that'll at least make up for Brother Brakebill leaving his wife for another man."

"I don't think my guy is coming with the right attitude," I warned.

"Your guy?" Walt turned to the others and laughed. "Once your new *boyfriend* steps into the church, he'll feel the Spirit, all right. He won't be able to help it." He laughed, and the others followed suit.

So immature.

The girls got in their car, the guys got in mine, and then we drove back to the ward meetinghouse on St. Charles so they could retrieve their own vehicles. I listened to Imagine Dragons on the way home. I loved the song "Demons." As if a Mormon singer would have any reason to know about such things.

"You smell like smoke," Mom said when I walked through the door. I didn't see how. There was no smoking in the bar, only a couple of men near the door after we walked out. But then, Mom always had a nose for sin. She'd caught me all three times I'd had a cup of coffee at Starbucks.

"You shouldn't have waited up," I replied. It was almost midnight.

"I can never rest until I know you're home safe."

I gave her a kiss on the cheek. She sniffed my shirt.

"Alcohol, too, Mort?" she asked with a raised eyebrow. Patrick must have spilled some. I hadn't noticed.

"It was a service project," I explained, telling her about the evening. She frowned the entire time I spoke.

"Don't tell your father," she said. "You know how he feels about transvestites and child molesters."

I shook my head, too weary to argue. If it hadn't been for the Word of Wisdom problems and all the sexuality, I could see how someone might actually have a good time at a bar. "Good night, Mom."

I stripped down to my garments and climbed into bed, forgetting to pray first. I slept soundly, though, but quite irritated to wake up the next day with a boner. Early morning erections took so long to go down, and I couldn't pee until they did.

I put on my white shirt and got ready for church, passing on Dad's offer to drive. I was too old to sit with my parents during Sacrament meeting. Besides, I had to pick up Patrick and so needed my own car. He was ready and waiting when I knocked on his door, even if he was wearing tan slacks and a green Polo shirt. I wasn't going to let that stop me, though.

Patrick's hand rested on my knee the whole drive Uptown. "You can't touch me at church," I warned. "There will be kids there."

Patrick nodded. "I can wait till after church at my place."

Our three-hour block was set up with Sacrament meeting first, then Sunday School, and finally Priesthood/Relief Society. Patrick never made a fuss the first two hours and didn't even look bored, though the youth speakers in Sacrament were awful and the Gospel Doctrine teacher clearly hadn't read the manual ahead of time.

It wasn't until the Elders Quorum met on stage in the Cultural Hall that I discovered bringing Patrick to church had been a mistake. To be honest, though, even when Walt first suggested the project, I hadn't felt any confirmation from the Holy Ghost.

Patrick stood up after the prayer and started passing out cards. "These have my name, phone number, and email address," he said. "If any of you have questions about gays or gay life, give me a call. I'm happy to talk to each of you personally. No judgments. You can ask me anything."

I saw Grant blush when he accepted the card, but he didn't crumple it or throw it on the stage like some of the other elders did. He put it in his pocket and looked at his Book of Mormon as if he expected it to spontaneously combust. Walt glared at me. Toby and Connor laughed. Boyd closed his eyes and seemed to be doing some kind of yoga.

"Maybe I'd better take you home, Patrick," I said, standing up. "Sorry, guys," I said to the rest of the group. Patrick looked unfazed.

"I—I'll go with you," Grant said. "You'll need a chaperone."

Patrick was decent enough not to laugh out loud, though the corners of his eyes crinkled.

I'd never met anyone with laugh lines before who hadn't been a good guy. Would he be the exception that proved the rule?

The three of us walked off the stage, with the other elders looking after us in disgust. I understood for the first time what gay men must feel almost every day. When I unlocked the car, Grant climbed into the back seat. I expected Patrick to sit in the front with me as he had on the way over and was surprised when he also sat in back. I pulled out and headed for the Marigny. No one said a word.

Grant stayed behind with Patrick when we stopped at the designated address. He somehow didn't even look Mormon anymore. There was something different about his expression. The Spirit must have left him. I shook his and Patrick's hands before I told them goodbye, my eyes fixed on a pot of daisies growing near Patrick's front door. A young white woman on a bicycle pedaled by. An older black woman walking her dog paused at a fire hydrant.

I passed the Moby Dick as I turned onto Elysian Fields and looked at its faded red walls. The place didn't look scary in the daylight, just old. Imagine Dragons sang "Believer."

Dad had picked up some Burger King on his way home from church. It meant conducting a commercial transaction, but it also meant Mom could rest on the Sabbath, so we had fast food almost every Sunday. Mom offered a blessing, and then we dug into our burgers and fries. Dad had even gotten us apple pie.

I didn't bring up Patrick or anything else that had transpired the last couple of days. But after I finished my last bite, I went to my room, pulled out my phone, and called Grant, leaving him a message saying I hoped we could still be friends.

Birds Don't Fly in the Rain

"The Family Council will now come to order." My father rapped a wooden gavel he'd bought at a thrift store on the end table beside his easy chair. I gritted my teeth. I'd never enjoyed these meetings, but they'd become downright intolerable since I'd told my parents eight months ago I was gay.

"Cindy," my father continued, "since you won last month's scoring, you get to say the opening prayer."

My sister stood up, folded her arms, and bowed her head. The rest of us followed suit. Except me. Once Cindy began, I looked up to watch the rest of my family. Mom was a little dowdy, only in her early forties but looking as if she'd been that age for a good fifteen years. My brothers and sisters ranged in age from eight to eighteen, my sister Marcia being the oldest. My father had petitioned the major networks to do a reality show based on our lives, but if we were a television series, I thought, we deserved to be canceled.

My father's name was Ken Brady, but his middle name was Michael, and when he married my mom, Caroline, they decided they would name their kids after the characters in *The Brady Bunch*. So my two brothers were named Greg and Bobby, my sisters were Marcia, Jan, and Cindy. I, of course, was Peter.

It was a miracle the six children were evenly divided between boys and girls, but my parents felt this was just Heavenly Father supporting their effort to create an ideal family. The fact that the sixth child born had been a fourth boy, and he'd died just hours after birth, only confirmed Heavenly Father's intervention and approval.

"Thank you, Cindy," my dad said when my sister finished. She returned to her seat. "Well, let's get right to business," he continued. "Here's the ranking for Greg." He pulled out a notebook and began reading. "Church attendance: 10. Obedience: 8. Spirituality: 6. Humility: 5. Fulfilling callings: 7."

He continued rating my brother on a scale of 1 to 10 in the remaining categories of Modesty, Scripture Reading, Willing Attitude, Missionary Work, and Word of Wisdom. I personally thought that adherence to the Word of Wisdom should fall under Obedience, as should some of the other categories, but Dad insisted that doing it his way allowed for a total of 100 points for someone with a perfect score.

I heard a crow outside squawking loudly. I loved crows. They were so good at problem solving.

Greg ended up with a final score of 79. He wasn't going to be champion this month. Cindy had won the past two months in a row, but no one stayed on top for long. Dad would arbitrarily change the score for any given child in a specific category, even if they'd performed equally well from one month to the next, just to keep everyone on their toes. The winner received their favorite dessert every Sunday until the next Family Council.

Not an incredible prize, but the loser at the bottom of the list received a penalty of far greater weight. He or she would have to mow the lawn every week for the following month, and clean the bathroom, and take out the trash. "It's just a taste of what life will be like for you if you don't reach the Celestial Kingdom."

Dad did occasionally seem to take pity on the youngest family members. They might come in fourth or fifth in the ranking, but they rarely came in last place and so didn't have to do the heavy tasks very often. But the danger was there, he reminded them almost nightly, so they tried to stay in line.

Even Mom came in last place once in a while. Dad seemed to take a special delight in that, but Mom had learned to soften him up the last week before Family Council by serving his favorite meals. She'd made stuffed artichokes last night, my dad's all-time favorite vegetable.

I personally didn't consider bread crumbs a vegetable.

Marcia was judged next. She was the only one in the family who helped me keep the hummingbird feeder clean and filled. Dad disapproved of our attempts to attract the tiny, beautiful birds. "If you keep feeding them," he said, "they'll never learn to make it on their own. They need to be able to fend for themselves or they'll become weak." But I was fascinated by their ability to survive at all, given their metabolism, and wanted to do whatever I could to make life better for them.

"A four!" Marcia interrupted our father. "Why do I only get a four in Humility?"

Dad looked down at his paper, scratched something out, and wrote again. "Challenging authority," he mumbled. "Your score is now a three in Humility."

Marcia clamped her lips shut and sat back, her arms folded tightly across her chest. Her final score was 75. Normally, I'd have been next in the queue, but Dad skipped over me for the time being and went directly to Jan. Jan was a Bird of Paradise, always wearing the brightest clothes she could find at the thrift store. She often wore scarves or hats or various brightly colored bits of costume jewelry.

At fourteen, she looked like an adult, and this usually counted against her during Family Council. While her clothes were completely in keeping with Mormon standards of chastity, Dad always gave her low marks for "attracting attention." Still, she ended up doing better than Marcia today, with a final score of 76.

Marcia had to be fuming about her lowered Humility score. "Jan always gets everything she wants," Marcia had complained to me one day. "It's always Jan, Jan, Jan."

The irony was lost on her. Marcia may have had a willing heart with the hummingbirds, but there were days when she didn't even seem as bright as the crows in our back yard. And days when she seemed equally as aggressive as the blue jay that swooped in to terrorize the wrens.

I'd seen her once deliberately stain Jan's favorite blouse with a drop of tomato sauce. Of course, Jan's response was to then carefully place stains on the rest of the blouse to make a pattern, happily wearing it anyway, infuriating Marcia all the more.

Bobby was next. He'd been caught breaking his fast too early on the most recent Fast Sunday, and he'd been caught another time with an old *Playboy* underneath his mattress. He was only ten years old. Dad didn't just calmly keep track of the offenses till the end of the month, though, to calculate Bobby's score.

He also punished Bobby almost daily for all his offenses, a spanking here, the withdrawal of television privileges there, an order to sit in the corner another time during Family Home Evening while wearing a dunce hat, whatever Dad thought it might take to whip the boy into shape.

Just yesterday, I'd caught Bobby pouring some salt into the bottom of Dad's shoes.

I didn't say anything. There was no category for Tattling. Or Getting Revenge.

Bobby and Cindy sometimes played "church." Bobby would be the bishop and Cindy would be Mom. Bobby would interview Cindy, and no matter how the interview went, he concluded with "Tell Brother Brady to come see me immediately. And tell him he'd better be ready to repent." Then they'd giggle and go on with their play. The day Dad overheard them, he sent them both to bed without their supper.

Bobby always reminded me of the passenger pigeon. Once, the sky had been filled with billions of them. But people kept shooting them, day after day after day. And finally, one day they were completely extinct. James Fenimore Cooper, the man who'd written *Last of the Mohicans*, had predicted their demise decades earlier, just because he could see what would happen if people continued their harmful behavior.

While I didn't think Dad would kill my younger brother, I still worried he might become extinct. Or at least that his independent, rebellious spirit might.

It was watching my younger brother behave so bravely in defiance of our father that finally gave me the courage to tell my folks I was gay back when I was fifteen. Wesley, my best friend from school, had warned me not to do it, but I wanted to be honest with them. I hadn't expected my parents to be happy about it, but I also hadn't expected Dad to forbid me from being ordained a priest when I turned sixteen.

I hadn't expected him to permanently forbid me from partaking of the sacrament with the rest of the congregation watching and wondering what terrible sins I'd committed. I hadn't expected him to force me to take up running. Every morning since my confession, Dad had driven me three miles from the house, dropped me off where there was no bus route, and forced me to run back to the house if I wanted to eat breakfast and pick up my books before school. Given the distance and the timing, the only way I could accomplish the task was by running at full speed.

I felt like a chicken, running, running, running, but never able to fly for very long.

Dad read out Bobby's score. Church attendance: 10. Obedience: 3. Spirituality: 4. Humility: 2. And so forth and so on. His final score was 43.

Cindy's score came to 78. She'd learned that playing church with Bobby didn't help her at Family Council and had given it up months ago. Bobby had taken to playing both the bishop *and* Dad and was still getting spanked when Dad overheard. Greg let out a whoop when Cindy's number was announced.

Dad gave him a stern look and he calmed down. Even though it was clear I wouldn't win, Mom had yet to undergo her judging, so his victory was premature. Sure enough, she came out with a score of 80. When Mom heard it, she let out a whoop as well and stuck her tongue out at Greg, who scowled in response.

Of course, there was still the matter of my score.

"So, Peter," Dad said slowly, "are you still gay?"

"Yes."

He nodded. "Then that's a zero for you in Obedience and Spirituality and Humility and Modesty and Willing Attitude." I could see Bobby calculating that the highest I could score if I received a perfect ten in every other category was only fifty. He breathed in relief.

But I did have a willing attitude. I was in fact modest and obedient. I never touched myself inappropriately. Well, almost never. And I prayed every day for Heavenly Father to make me straight. I knew I'd never marry a woman if I couldn't change, and I knew I'd never allow myself to be with a man, either. I was committed to a life of celibacy if it came to that.

Didn't that earn me at least a two?

"Peter gets a ten for church attendance but only a five for fulfilling his callings. Since he isn't ordained a priest, he isn't blessing the sacrament every Sunday like he's supposed to. He only gets a six in Scripture Reading because he's obviously not reading with the proper attitude."

These categories seemed awfully fuzzy, I thought. Wasn't "proper attitude" the same as "willing attitude"? I tried to keep my face blank.

But at this point, Bobby stood up and did a little jig. Dad ignored him and continued tallying up my points. "Final score: 33." He sighed heavily. "Too bad it wasn't your other brother who lived."

I felt my face go hot even as my chest went cold. I thought of the book I was secretly reading in the public library without checking it out. *Toward a Mormon Worldview*. The cover featured a photo of two men and a woman, all kneeling on the ground with their heads buried in the sand.

"I want to change my score," I said.

"Certainly," Dad agreed. "Change your behavior and I'll change your score. Next month. You're in last place this month. Again."

"I have some new information that will affect my scoring *this* month," I insisted.

"Yes?" Dad frowned. "I'll consider it, but I won't make any promises." Bobby was frowning as well.

"You gave me an eight in Word of Wisdom."

"That's because you had that one Coke."

"But that's not the only thing I drank."

Dad's frown deepened. "You're asking me to *lower* your score?"

I walked over and whispered into his ear. "Is it against the Word of Wisdom to drink semen?" I asked.

Of course, I'd never done any such thing, mine or anyone else's. But I just couldn't bear listening to this man any longer. He jumped out of his chair, almost knocking me over, and pointed to the hallway. "Go to your room!" he bellowed.

I went, hoping that maybe now the rest of the family might discuss whether they should place me in foster care. I knew Dad was torn between having others think we were the perfect family and getting me out of his life. I thought of Robert Reed, who'd died of AIDS. I thought of Florence Henderson, who'd recently died as well.

I felt like the last Dodo bird in existence.

And I *was* a dodo. Wesley had known I was gay even before I said anything and didn't care. When he'd told his parents a few months ago about my father forcing me to run every morning, they offered to take me in. I'd dismissed the offer as unnecessary, but now I wondered if they'd still be willing.

Several bird species were known to adopt chicks of other parents, sometimes even of other species altogether.

There might have been a brief window of opportunity with Wesley that was now closed, but it was worth a shot. And if Wesley's parents had in fact changed their minds, I'd go ahead and talk to a school counselor about foster care. I doubted Dad would put up much of a fight, and Mom always did whatever Dad said. If worse came to worst, he could always take in some foster child himself, another boy named Peter.

I wondered if I should walk back to the living room and tell my dad that the final score I gave *him* was a big, fat goose egg. Instead, I looked out my bedroom window to the tree in our back yard and watched two crows grooming each other on one of the higher branches.

Such beautiful creatures. They mourned when one of their own was lost. They remembered the faces of humans who'd hurt them.

I went to my bookcase, grabbed my copy of Hitchcock's *The Birds*, and slipped it into the DVD player. I leaned back against my pillow and hit Play.

A Mormon in Morocco

"Thank you for walking me to my door, Abbou," I said, slipping my key in the lock.

"We shouldn't have stayed out this late," Abbou replied.

I swung the door open and stepped inside, turning around to face my friend. "Would you like to come in?"

Abbou smiled. "Grace, you know that's not a good idea. It should have been a woman walking you to your door to begin with. Don't make things worse."

"Oh, Abbou, I don't care what people think. Besides, then she would have had to go home without an escort herself."

"You shouldn't be living alone in the first place. You should have a woman roommate or two. Or three. And you should take more care about what people think, Grace. You should."

While I was of Lebanese descent, my heritage was Christian, Mormon the last two generations, and I knew almost nothing about Muslim culture. I expected it varied a bit from country to country. That was one thing in its favor. Mormons were tediously the same almost everywhere one went.

I'd been in Morocco three months now, teaching English. I'd wanted to get as far away from Salt Lake as possible. Constant talk of temple marriage and bringing babies into the world. Neverending discussions of following the Spirit as I made life decisions. Ceaseless comments about our special place in the world. What we hoped to do in the Millennium. And beyond.

Sex with Abbou would help deflect all that. "I'd like you to come in," I said.

Abbou looked toward the neighbor's apartment, but the door was closed. I could see him calculating for a moment before he strode in quickly and shut the door behind him. "This can only help my reputation," he said, "but it'll do nothing except hurt yours."

"I'm American," I said. "Everyone expects me to be different from the other girls in Marrakech."

"It's better that you don't tell anyone about this."

"Not even Mariem?" Mariem was my best friend, another teacher at the school. She was also Abbou's sister, which was how we met. Mariem and I talked about everything. How our mothers were overbearing. Countries we'd like to visit. Which Moroccan actors we liked best.

Abbou debated for a moment and then shook his head. "No one," he repeated.

In a way, the secrecy made Abbou's presence even sexier. He'd never expressed any interest in me, but I figured that was just because I was his sister's friend and he was being "proper." I was reasonably attractive, at least by American standards— green eyes, two dimples, and luxurious black hair.

Not that Abbou had been able to see much of my hair, given that I always wore my hijab in public. But I couldn't bring myself to wear a veil like so many of the other women did here. With the government banning full face veils recently, that practice was thankfully going away, though not fast enough.

"Let me make some tea," I said.

"We don't have time for tea. Let's just do what you have in mind."

I laughed. "First, you're worried about my reputation, and now you can't get to the bedroom fast enough?"

Abbou grinned. "I really like you, Grace, but we're not going to date. My family would never allow it."

"But they'll allow you to have sex with me?"

Abbou's smile faded.

"I'm sorry. Don't worry about it. Yes, I'd like to have sex with you. I appreciate you being so accommodating." I led Abbou to the tiny bedroom. At twenty-five, I was still a virgin. I'd earned my English degree from Brigham Young University and served a mission in Greece. Neither venture had been as fulfilling as I'd hoped. And now I was in Morocco teaching English for a year. Maybe longer, if I continued to enjoy myself.

I pulled down the bedclothes. Abbou began unbuttoning his shirt. I slipped off my hijab and started unbuttoning my shirt.

Twenty minutes later, it was all finished. While Abbou was perhaps a year older than I and in wonderful shape, I didn't find the sex as satisfying as I'd believed it would be. Was every major milestone in my life destined to feel so empty? Something must be wrong with me. People always made such a fuss about sex. But then, maybe the problem was that Abbou was telling the truth. He really wasn't that into me. In fact, he was sitting on the edge of the bed now, looking depressed.

God, was I that bad? With no experience, I didn't know.

"Thank you, Abbou. I appreciate it."

"Stop using that word!" He covered his ears.

I put on my nightgown and sat beside him, so brown and naked. He looked at me sadly and shook his head. "I've defiled you."

"I'm the same person I was half an hour ago," I said.

"No, you're not. And neither am I."

I thought it was always the woman who regretted sex. "We can go back to just being friends, can't we? Just being together when Mariem is with us?"

"I've got to leave." Abbou stood and began pulling his clothes back on. He was certainly beautiful. But he was probably right about me needing to keep a low profile. I wouldn't be able to ask another man over to my place for several more months. As lackluster as the event had been, I wasn't totally put off by that.

"You don't belong here, Grace. You should go back to America."

I supposed he might have a point. It wasn't as if I needed to live in Salt Lake, was it? I could move to Los Angeles or Chicago or New York. Living a secret life in Salt Lake simply sounded depressing. Living one in Miami sounded average. And there was nothing wrong with average. It was just that living one here sounded thrilling.

I peeked out to make sure no neighbors were in the hallway, a little disappointed to see it empty, and let Abbou slip out quietly. I locked the door and then sat on my sofa to think. I wanted to celebrate, but I obviously couldn't go out to have a drink. Not that I had the money to do anything so extravagant in the first place. I only earned about $950 a month—all in dirham, of course—and rent with utilities cost almost $850.

If I hadn't saved up a little money before coming here, I'd be living a stark life indeed. But there'd be no point in making a bigger salary since it was against the law to send money out of the country. Dirham couldn't even be exchanged outside of Morocco, only in the airport as one left. I could use my credit card here, but I could only pay it by transferring funds from my U.S. account.

I felt I should read something from the Book of Mormon after my experience with Abbou, but I'd deliberately not brought one into the country. Mariem had given me a copy of the Quran, telling me it would be useful to be familiar with it, but I didn't want to read that, either. I needed to do something, though, perhaps get away to Rabat for a few days. Life was so much less hectic there. Maybe I could do some serious reflecting. The train wouldn't cost much. The mountains would be nice, too. Couldn't go very far east, though, since the border with Algeria was closed. No, Rabat sounded like the best bet.

I just hated traveling alone. Women were subject to such harassment without a chaperone. I wondered if I could ask Mariem to come with me. It would be hard to spend so much time with her, though, and not mention her brother.

The next day at work, I suggested the trip to Mariem. "Abbou told me what happened," she said. So much for keeping everything a secret. "I should be mad at you."

"But you aren't?"

"Considering the situation, no."

I wasn't sure what that meant but figured it was best not to pursue the point. "So you'll come?"

She shook her head. "No, Grace, I think you need some time to yourself." She frowned. "And I mean time *alone*. I don't think you appreciate the grief that could come your way."

I wanted to say we weren't all like the women portrayed on American television, but Mariem had never seen any American shows, so that wouldn't have helped. And maybe I was more like them than I thought. Moroccan television did air some heavily censored U.S. programs, but Mariem had been forbidden from watching them in any event. "Let me treat you to a Poms," I said. I'd learned early on not to buy water from water sellers.

"No, but I will walk with you to the train station so you can buy your ticket."

"Thanks, Mariem."

The next morning, I was on a train to the capital. The car was hot and crowded. I sat next to two women, Chafika and Inaya, who smiled as they introduced themselves and offered me dried apricots. Both women were in their late twenties, both probably thirty pounds overweight. They were waitresses in Marrakech, where they were harassed daily by the customers, so they liked to go off together when they could afford it and enjoy a break.

Chafika sported a bold, prominent nose which somehow made her seem the leader of the two. Inaya possessed a receding chin.

Many folks here could be quite reticent, but the two women spent an hour telling me about their similar childhoods, their families, their favorite singers, even their favorite constellations. In return, they asked specific questions about my life in a way that led me to feel I'd better edit heavily or risk offending them.

I had years of practice at those kinds of answers and responded accordingly. Despite the self-censoring, I enjoyed our conversation and felt saddened as we approached Rabat.

"Do you have a hotel room?" Chafika asked.

I hadn't been expecting that question. "Not yet."

"Then stay with us. You'll be safer. And it'll be cheaper for all of us."

The hotel was modest, but certainly as good as anything I might have been able to afford on my own. There was only one bed, but there was also a soft chair. "We can all fit." Inaya pointed to the bed, but I shook my head.

We ate dinner at an inexpensive restaurant nearby. I ordered the tajine while both Chafika and Inaya ordered couscous. "Why something so bland?" I asked.

"It's fattening." Inaya giggled.

"I'm such a good cook," Chafika said, confident without boasting, "that I'm often disappointed by anything but the simplest of dishes, which you can hardly ruin."

"We want to open our own restaurant one day," Inaya added. "Chafika is great with b'ssara and makouda and zaalouk and b'stilla. And she makes a great harira for Ramadan."

Chafika stared into her couscous. "If only women could do things like own restaurants," she said softly. Then she looked up and smiled. "What do you want to do when you go back to America?" she asked.

I shrugged. "Teach, I guess."

Chafika's face fell. "Nothing more…important?"

"I think teaching is very important," I said, my tone a little defensive.

Perhaps they were self-censoring around me.

"It's just that women can do that even here. Don't you want to do something you can't do anywhere else?"

I frowned. "Like be CEO of a bank or something?"

Both women nodded.

"I don't want to be a CEO."

Chafika and Inaya looked at each other. Then Chafika shrugged. "Maybe the men are right," she said. "Even what I want to do is basically be a glorified housewife. That's all cooking is."

The conversation drifted on to other topics, but I couldn't stop thinking about what the women had said. I'd come to Morocco to find myself, and it was disturbing to think I was finding that all I wanted from life was what Mormonism offered me in the first place. A "supportive" place in society. To be good at my womanly role. Why didn't I want to be a museum director? An archeologist? A symphony conductor?

These two plump women in traditional Muslim garb looked more liberated than I felt.

But I'd had sex, hadn't I? I did my shopping alone most days. I was a wild woman.

After we finished our meal, we went back to the hotel to make plans for the following day. The beaches in Rabat were polluted and contaminated, so there was little point going there, though lots of people did. Skipping the beach was disappointing, but it wasn't as if I had a bathing suit I could wear anyway. I'd planned on picking something modest up here.

Chafika suggested shopping among the street vendors for scarves and other items of clothing. It didn't sound like the self-reflective trip I'd been hoping for, and I wondered if there was any polite way to ditch the two women for a few hours the next day and stroll around by myself. For liberated women, they weren't very exciting. But it didn't hurt to have bodyguards in a strange city.

I was less exciting than they were and I knew it.

"You sure you don't want to join us in the bed?" Chafika asked when it was time to call it a night.

"No, I'm good." I pulled a light wrap over me in the chair.

Inaya turned out the lamp, though there was still light from the street streaming in through the window. The streets weren't as noisy as those in Marrakech, so I was still able to fall asleep. But at some point not long after, I was awakened by a noise I hadn't expected.

Chafika and Inaya were kissing. I could hear them moaning lightly. Oh, my lord. Did they think I was lesbian, too? Is that why they invited me to stay with them? There was no way to tune them out, and the sounds only grew louder. I could see movement in the darkness, a thin beam of light striking the foot of the bed, its shape continually shifting. At one point, I heard Chafika saying, "You can come join us, Grace, if you want."

I didn't say anything, and they continued as they were.

When it was all finally done, I felt exhausted. I hadn't realized I was expending so much energy wishing for it all to be over. Inaya turned on the lamp. "You look unhappy. We didn't upset you, did we? I thought you were one of us."

I wasn't sure if I was offended or not. "I like men," I said, to make my position clear.

"I can't imagine why," said Chafika. "Moroccan men are awful."

I thought of Abbou. I didn't suppose I wanted to marry him, but I would have liked him to like me.

"We had to gain some weight so we'd have an excuse for not going out with men," Chafika continued. "We can tell our family no one is asking us out. But you'd be surprised how many old, fat men still find us attractive."

"I still find you attractive," said Inaya.

"I just wish King Mohammed—"

"Don't say anything about the king," Inaya cut her off.

"All I was going to say was—"

"Do you want to go to prison?" Inaya looked about the room as if expecting someone to come out from behind the curtains.

"Okay, okay. I just wish we didn't have to worry about men."

"Why don't you go to America?" I asked.

Chafika and Inaya laughed. "I love your sense of humor. It's too bad you aren't one of us. I really thought you might be."

"You can't imagine how terrifying it was the first time we expressed our feelings. If our families found out…"

"The law here…"

I felt a chill and pulled my wrap more tightly about my neck.

I didn't tell them that Mormon families weren't much more understanding about homosexuality or even such benign things as coffee and tea. The only reason my parents had "allowed" me to come here was because they felt I'd be obligated to follow the same standard of chastity that I did in Utah.

I never even masturbated until I came to Marrakech.

"You sure you don't want to hop in bed for a little bit?"

I shook my head. "It's not on my bucket list."

We spent the next day roaming the little shops around Rabat. I bought a couple of scarves just to feel I was making the trip worthwhile, though these were items I could have picked up in Marrakech just as easily. Chafika bought some spices, and Inaya bought a long skirt.

I wished Abbou had at least wanted an affair. I wished I hadn't made him feel so compromised.

Chafika picked out a restaurant for us again that evening, and she and Inaya ordered couscous once more while I tried something more adventurous. A group of four men asked if we needed escorts back to our apartment. Chafika told them our escorts were already on the way. When the three of us reached the hotel room, I endured another lovemaking session by streetlight. I wished I'd brought some headphones.

Then the next morning, we were off to the train station to head back to Marrakech. Chafika insisted I come sometime to the restaurant where she worked, and I agreed. I did like the two well enough, I supposed. And lesbians weren't quite as boring as other women. If only because they'd proven they could think outside the box to some degree.

Perhaps they were unorthodox in other ways as well, though I suspected lesbians could succeed at being as boring as anyone else if they tried. Still, I hoped I could live a little adventurously through them. I called Mariem, but she didn't answer. I wished I could call Abbou. Surely, if I got better at sex, he'd like me.

Back at work the following day, Mariem kept avoiding me, but I finally cornered her as classes were letting out. "Mariem!" I said when I saw her up close. "What's wrong? What happened?"

"You happened."

I frowned. "What do you mean?"

"Abbou told his boyfriend about what you two did, and his boyfriend broke up with him."

"His boyfriend! That's funny, because—"

"Abbou was telling me about it, crying and crying, and our brother Darid overheard." She closed her eyes for a moment. "Then he told our other brother Namir."

I could feel my throat constricting. "Mariem…"

"They tortured him."

"Oh!" This was like something out of a horror movie. Like *Argo* or *A Mighty Heart*. She had to be making it up to put me in my place.

"And then they killed him. For bringing shame upon our family."

"Mariem!" This couldn't be real. Things like this didn't really happen. Not really. Not so suddenly. Even Mormons only stopped inviting you to Christmas dinners.

I'd just touched Abbou's beautiful skin a few days ago. A few hours, it seemed. He'd been so gentle. That was probably even why I hadn't been more aroused. I wanted—

I thought of one of our fellow teachers who'd been killed by her father when she became pregnant while still unmarried. I remembered the woman a street over who was considered "easy" by her neighbors, and how after being raped by three men, the police didn't even bother arresting them. I remembered the article in the newspaper about how women could use makeup to hide signs of abuse and "get on with their lives."

What had I been thinking?

Poor, sweet Abbou, who didn't even much like me.

"I do not wish to be friends with you anymore, Grace." Mariem turned and walked away without another word.

I strolled back to my apartment alone, paying no attention to the others around me on the street, unsure if anyone was even noticing my new scarf, but sure they could see the stain on my soul. I should go back to Salt Lake, I told myself, sitting at my living room window and looking out over the street. I could have a life there. I could work with immigrant women, help them adjust to American culture.

Another "supportive" role.

I looked up flights to the U.S. and stared out my window a while longer. Finally, I fixed my scarf and walked out the door, walking alone to the restaurant where Chafika and Inaya worked. I ignored the people who looked at me askance. I sat down at a table and waited for Chafika to take my order.

I would help these women get to America, if that's what they wanted.

But not Salt Lake.

"So good to see you again," Chafika said.

"Can you recommend anything?" I asked. "The couscous?" I tried to smile.

"The pigeon pastry here is good."

I nodded and ordered the b'stilla. When Chafika delivered it a few minutes later, I handed her a slip of paper with my address and phone number. She smiled and tucked it into a pocket. I ate my meal in silence, paid my bill, and walked back to my apartment alone.

Bread and Pottage

The doorbell rang and I gave Craig a quick kiss. He didn't kiss me back. "It's the missionaries," I said. "Gotta go."

Craig gave a resigned nod and squeezed my hand, an odd gesture of intimacy given the lack of the kiss, but I was grateful for anything I got these days. "I hope you hear back from the bank soon."

"Too bad there's no god to ask for help."

"Oh, Devin."

I opened the front door to find Elders Crumholt and Sawyer on the front steps. They were the missionaries who'd baptized me two months ago, attractive men maybe ten years younger than I was. I still knew almost nothing about Mormonism, only that in exchange for one delivery of welfare food a month, there seemed to be an awfully large number of strings attached. "Hey, Elders," I said, "good to see you."

"Hi, Brother Weaver. Ready to go teach tonight? Ready to bear your testimony?"

"Always prepared to serve the Lord," I replied. I almost shouted out, "Bye, hon" to my former husband but caught myself in time. Craig had been nothing but supportive since I lost my job at the bank, even taking extra overtime when he could, but there were plenty of signs he wasn't okay.

He spent more time with friends now than before. He'd sit down alone to DVDs we had planned to watch together. And he beat off loudly in the bathroom so I'd be perfectly aware he wasn't devoting any of his sex to me.

So maybe he wasn't entirely supportive.

I followed the elders out to their car, and we took off for Brad Thatcher's house. Only seventeen, he still lived with his parents and siblings. Our goal was to get him to commit to serving a mission when he turned eighteen in four months.

"Any luck finding a full-time job?" Elder Crumholt asked, glancing up at me in the rearview mirror.

"Still have just the part-time job the Ward Employment Specialist found for me."

"The Lord tries those he loves."

"I could do with a little less love."

"Oh, don't say that! It's *good* to suffer. It's only by overcoming adversity that we get a chance at the Celestial Kingdom. I'm sure that's why Heavenly Father makes so many people gay."

Craig and I had recently checked *Stonewall* out from the library. I was running an errand and missed the beginning but was mesmerized by the part I did see. No one, of course, would be making a movie about me selling my soul for a little food.

When we arrived at the Thatchers' house, I followed behind Elder Crumholt and Elder Sawyer. I wished I'd refused to come. I wished I could duck around the corner and hide. But there was no hiding in the Mormon Church. If the elders weren't reporting on me to the bishop, then my Home Teachers were.

If only Craig and I could get by on his income alone. We'd tried for five months, but we simply couldn't make ends meet. He'd gotten the loan on his house before we even met, but somehow, living there just cost more now. We missed a Visa payment. Then a cable bill. And then we were a week late with the mortgage payment.

That's when I came up with the idea to call the missionaries and convert. The information I'd heard about the Church Welfare program wasn't completely accurate, though. The bishop refused to help with actual money.

"Since the house is in your friend's name, there's nothing we can do."

"The electricity's in my name. Can you help with that?"

"Let's have you make an appointment to see the Ward Employment Specialist."

So now I had a part-time job installing attic insulation. Impossible to turn down without having my welfare cut off. And infuriating to have to pay tithing on it or still be refused the food delivery.

"Good evening, Elders," said Brother Thatcher. "Brad's in the living room with Sister Thatcher. Come on in." We joined the others. Everyone shook hands and sat down. There was a Wii console on the end table next to a book by Boyd K. Packer.

"So, Brad," Elder Crumholt said, "have you been praying and fasting about what we talked about last time?"

Brad nodded glumly.

"Why don't you start us off tonight with a prayer?" Elder Crumholt continued. We all bowed our heads while Brad mumbled a short prayer. "Have you made a decision about your mission yet?" Elder Crumholt went on after Brad finished.

Brad shook his head.

"Brad, I can't emphasize enough what an incredible opportunity it is to serve the Lord," Elder Crumholt blathered on. I really felt for the kid. "You have the chance to meet great people. You have the chance to learn about yourself and the world. You have the chance to watch people change their lives for the better." Here he motioned to me. "Brother Weaver was living in sin when we found him. He was gay, just like you think you are. And even though Brother Weaver was legally married to another man, he repented and chose to follow the Savior." Elder Crumholt nodded for me to take over the story.

"I divorced my husband," I said. "I chose to live a celibate life. I know first-hand that obeying the commandments is more fulfilling than a life of depravity."

This is what selling one's soul felt like. Not pushing car loans on customers who didn't need them. Not pushing high interest credit cards. Not the one time I cheated on my husband.

I remembered the day Craig proposed. We were walking along the sidewalk near his house, picking blackberries from the bushes that grew like weeds throughout that area of Boulder. Craig had popped a fresh blackberry into my mouth and said, "Will you pick blackberries with me for the rest of my life?"

I'd put a blackberry in his mouth and said yes.

Craig wouldn't eat the blackberry jam I received from the Bishop's Storehouse.

Brad looked at me, his gaze so intense I could feel it boring into me. I wanted to tell this kid it was okay to lie, to tell his parents what they wanted to hear until they finished paying for his education, and then come out and live the life he wanted. But, of course, if I said such a thing, I'd be excommunicated and lose my food allowance.

Even Joseph Smith kept secrets.

I didn't learn that from the missionaries.

"Dad says you still live with your ex-husband." Brad spoke so softly I could barely hear him.

"We live in separate rooms now," I said. "I couldn't afford a place of my own, and…" I didn't want to tell him that the bishop had said it was better for me to live with an openly gay man than it was for him to spend the Lord's money unwisely on unnecessary rent. Explaining that made me sound ungrateful. And I wasn't. I liked still living with Craig.

Most of the time.

"Do you really not like guys anymore?" Brad asked, the tips of his ears turning red. His mother closed her eyes and looked like she was trying not to notice she was still in the room.

"It's all a spectrum," I said. "I'll always like guys *some*. I've just learned to love the Lord *more*. I get more happiness from following Heavenly Father than I ever got from any relationship with any man *ever*."

Thank God there was no god to punish me for lying.

If only the Employment Specialist could help me learn to perform better in job interviews. I was a great employee. I just sucked at interviews. You could only be rejected so many times before you began believing you were a piece of crap.

"Brad," I said, "two years seems like a long time right now, but I can tell you that it'll fly by. Even if you were straight, you wouldn't want to get married right out of high school. So there's no reason not to put off dating a couple more years. If you go on a mission, you might end up in Japan or New Zealand. It could be a great adventure. And even if you only end up in someplace like Oregon, it's still a great opportunity to see what other parts of the U.S. are like. It gives you options. You can always leave the Church when you get back. But give it a shot first."

"What if…what if I fall in love with my companion?" Brad looked at the floor. I saw Elders Crumholt and Sawyer exchange nervous glances.

"You deal with that when it happens." It was clear I wasn't only selling my own soul. I was encouraging this young man to sell his as well.

How awful to be a missionary. Selling self-loathing. Why anyone had to buy something that one could usually obtain for free I didn't know.

I'd grown up in a non-religious family with two professors for parents, so there'd been no homophobia to speak of, and coming out hadn't been the ordeal it clearly was for Brad. My big resentment toward the parental units came in regard to Santa. My folks always told me the sainted figure was made up, and I remembered being upset that other kids got to believe while I didn't.

I still felt a flash of irritation every year around Christmastime for all the magic I'd missed. If such a stupid thing as that was going to haunt me the rest of my life, I couldn't imagine what Brad was facing, even if he did eventually come out completely.

And I was only making it worse.

I felt like a Jewish kapo in the camps.

Maybe Craig should sell the house so we could find a one-bedroom apartment. I was still reasonably young and good looking. I could sell myself to other men. It would be less degrading than what I was doing now.

I had to do a lot of volunteer work at the church, serving as ward librarian and substitute Sunday pianist. The jobs themselves weren't terribly degrading, but the fact that I *had* to do them or have my food cut off was. Why couldn't these people just be nice to me without demanding something in return? There never seemed to be any time to enjoy Craig's company anymore, the times he was still at home.

Of course, I liked playing the piano again. Craig and I had had to sell ours. My husband—my *ex*-husband—was feeling so much financial stress we'd stopped having sex long before I called the missionaries. I wished that instead of ordering me to divorce, the bishop had offered us counseling on how to survive financial difficulty in a relationship.

The elders, Brad, and I talked some more while Brad's parents sat silently, their lips sometimes moving as if they were praying while we talked. At one point, Brother Thatcher cleared his throat. "Why do you think this happened to our son?" he asked. He looked as if he was about to put his hand on Brad's shoulder, but he pulled back at the last moment.

"There's no reason," I said. "Some people are just gay."

"But I saw a report that the oceans are getting warmer and it's making some dolphins turn gay."

My mouth fell open. I almost said, "I hope it's the cute dolphins that are turning," but fortunately stopped myself in time.

"We might have to give in to this global warming battle if it's turning people gay," Brother Thatcher said. "I turned down the AC here in the house a couple of degrees to see if that'll help Brad any." He glanced over at his wife. "Suggested to the bishop he turn down the air in the chapel, too. The women always seem to complain, but we need to do what we can to save our youth."

I didn't tell him I loved the cold and always had. In the winter, Craig and I kept the house at 60 degrees.

There was a little more chatting, ruminations about where Brad might be called to serve. Finally, though, Elder Crumholt asked his companion to offer a closing prayer, and then we all stood. "Brad, we'll stop by again next week to talk about this some more. Write a list of absolutely any questions you have either for us as missionaries or for Brother Weaver as a former gay man." Brad nodded mutely, and the elders and I headed back for the car.

"You did good, Brother Weaver," said Elder Crumholt as we took off.

"You be sure and tell the bishop," I said.

"Of course, of course."

We drove the rest of the way back to Craig's house in silence. I wasn't sure what the elders were thinking. I only knew that bank job or no bank job, I couldn't keep this up much longer.

I hoped. Was there a point of no return past which it was impossible to reclaim one's soul no matter how hard one tried? Surely, the pawn ticket expired at some point. Or was it simply that it had already been redeemed by someone else?

We pulled up in front of the house, and I grabbed the door handle. "Brother Weaver," said Elder Crumholt.

"Yes?" I was a little irritated. He'd had plenty of time to talk on the way home. I wanted to hold Craig again. Maybe I could talk him into it tonight. I hoped that would make me feel a little less dirty.

"Are you a top or a bottom?"

"Uh…"

"Can you be both?"

"Uh…"

"Th-the first time you had a man's penis inside you, what were you thinking?"

"Elder Crumholt," I said, "I don't think this is an appropriate conversation."

"I want to know, too," said Elder Sawyer.

"We tried it last night," Elder Crumholt continued. "We didn't have sex, of course! I just put my penis inside Elder Sawyer, and he put his inside me. We were curious."

Oh my God. If the bishop found out I'd corrupted the missionaries, my food allowance would be cut off for sure. "The question," I said, "isn't what *I* was thinking. What were *you* thinking?"

"It was better than Companion Inventory," Elder Crumholt said.

"It was even better than Dual Study," said Elder Sawyer.

"So we just wanted to know…"

"Yes?"

"…if it loses its charm. I mean, you willingly divorced your husband. I don't want to come out as gay, get excommunicated, and then find out five years from now it wasn't worth it."

Fast and Testimony meeting was coming up next week. I wished more than anything I could stand up and tell everyone my love for Craig was stronger than the power of their church. That giving up love made a person feel emptier than a few missed meals ever could. They'd cast me out, but maybe that would make up a little for letting them use me to beat down other gay members.

I wished…

"Elders, can I get back to you on this?" I asked. "Why don't you stop by tomorrow night? We can watch a movie and chat. I'll have Craig join us."

"Is 6:30 okay?" There was an eager note in Elder Crumholt's voice.

"Yes. We'll see you at 6:30." I thought of the last of the food allowance still in the refrigerator. "We'll have dinner first."

I climbed out of the car and watched the elders drive away. Then I trudged slowly up the walk and inserted my key into the lock. Craig was on the sofa watching *Wonder Woman*. I'd checked it out of the library this afternoon. We had planned to watch it together.

I picked up the remote and hit Pause.

"You have a good evening, Devin?"

I nodded. "But I want a better night."

Craig frowned.

"I want you back."

"After you get a job—"

"I want you back now."

"We're getting further behind on our bills every month as it is. You're doing the right thing."

For the first time, I realized he was lying to me the way I was lying to the bishop.

"I have nothing to offer you, Craig," I said, "except the likelihood you'll have to sell your house." I sighed. "I'm sorry."

"For what?"

"For losing my job, for one. But mostly, for thinking that having food on the table was more important than having you by my side."

"Well…"

"Can I ask you a favor, sweetie?"

Craig looked at me carefully.

"Will you baptize me back into gay life?"

Craig laughed. I realized it had been quite a while since the last time I'd heard that sound. "And just how am I supposed to do that?"

I shrugged. "Let's go to the bathhouse where we first met. You can dunk me in the hot tub. Then we can have wild, crazy sex."

"With each other," he clarified.

"With each other."

"What about the food allowance?"

"If I stop paying tithing, we can get groceries with the money from installing insulation until I find a full-time job again."

"So we'll get remarried as soon as we can afford the license?"

I nodded. I sure hoped I found a job with benefits that included counseling.

Craig leaned over and gave me a kiss. "I'll go put on my bathhouse clothes."

While he ran to the bedroom, I walked to the kitchen and prepared us each a slice of toast covered with blackberry jam. We gobbled it down, kissed like schoolboys, and hurried out to the car.

Stuck Up

"Roderick, you are so stuck up," Deanna said as she hung up the phone.

Just because I wouldn't ask her out. I couldn't complain, though. I'd deliberately cultivated that impression to give myself an excuse for not going out with girls. Even my male friends thought I was arrogant, simply because I said I wanted to go to law school after I earned my undergraduate degree. Because I said I wanted to marry a doctor.

"Money and prestige are more important to you than having a wife who wants to be a good mother?" demanded Levi, who'd turned eighteen a few days before I did. He was waiting for his mission call, while I hadn't sent my papers in yet. I might still turn them in and see if I had a chance to go somewhere like Iceland or Hungary. I could always turn down the call if I couldn't bear the location.

But I couldn't worry about any of that now. My parents had left this morning for Denmark to pick up my brother Samuel, who was just finishing his mission. They'd be gone for two weeks. As the youngest sibling and the only one still at home, I had the house to myself. That meant I could finally have sex for the first time.

I didn't want to make any decisions about a mission until I knew what I'd be missing. While it was still a terrible stigma among Bakersfield Mormons not to go on a mission, more and more young men were refusing a call these days, and more than a few were coming home early, even if they did initially accept. My fate wasn't sealed yet.

I jumped in the shower and cleaned myself better than I had in ages. I even stuck a soapy finger up my butt to make sure I was reasonably clean inside. While I knew I wanted to suck someone's member for a bit, what I really wanted was for another man to enter me. I'd been fantasizing about it for the past six years. I brushed my teeth, put on a clean pair of jeans with a neon green T-shirt, and headed out of the house. I had the use of Samuel's car while he was away. That privilege would soon be over.

All privileges might soon be over. If I didn't serve a mission, I certainly didn't want to attend Brigham Young University, and I wasn't sure my parents would pay for any other college.

I drove down to a seedy part of town and parked, walking the last two blocks to the Tail Pipe carefully. I didn't want to be mugged before I had my first sex. I wanted that dangling carrot. I showed my ID to a man at the door, and he stamped something on my hand, a signal, most likely, for the bartender not to serve me alcohol. There was no danger of that in any event. I didn't want to break the Word of Wisdom.

The bar was crowded with men in their twenties and thirties, a few men even in their forties. Since I'd always liked older men, I tried to position myself near one of them. Guys were talking and drinking and laughing. And ignoring me. There was no way I could approach someone else, though, not this soon, so I kept sipping my 7-Up and trying to catch another man's attention.

An hour passed, and I began to worry this might not happen tonight. I didn't suppose it *had* to, of course. I still had several more days. Another fifteen minutes passed. Standing around in a bar was boring. This wasn't at all the way I'd imagined it.

I was just about to call it a night when I felt someone touch my arm. I looked up and saw a good-looking man with dark hair. A good-looking older man, at least forty-five. I smiled. "My name's Alfonso," he said. "Alfonso Calderon." He held out his hand.

"Roderick Rasmussen," I replied. A handshake had never felt so sensual.

"I haven't seen you before. You new?"

I nodded.

"I love newbies," he went on. "They have so much more…enthusiasm."

"I'm a virgin," I blurted out, though I wasn't sure that was a selling point.

Without another word, Alfonso leaned into me, parting my lips with his tongue and sliding his own deep into my mouth. Now I understood why everyone wanted to make it to the Celestial Kingdom. If sex wasn't permitted in the lower kingdoms, kissing probably wasn't, either.

And what if sex was even better than this?

"I'd love to be your first," Alfonso said, "but I can't bring you to my place."

Was he married, I wondered? To either a man or a woman? This should matter to me, I thought, but right now, it didn't seem to. "You can come to my house."

Alfonso smiled. Outside, I explained the directions, and then I let him follow me in his car. I was mildly worried what the neighbors might think if they noticed a strange vehicle in front of our house, but it was almost midnight. Probably no one in the area would be up. I unlocked the door and ushered Alfonso inside.

"What's with the bag?" I asked.

"I always bring my own supplies." When I raised an eyebrow, he continued. "You know, condoms, lube, poppers."

"Poppers?"

Alfonso laughed. "You sniff them. Gives you a high."

"Oh, I don't think I'll use any of that."

Alfonso laughed again. "I didn't offer. They're mine."

I wasn't sure what the etiquette was for a one-night stand. Should I hand him a glass of water? Give him a tour of the house? Get on my knees right here in the living room, or take him straight to my bedroom?

"Which way?" asked Alfonso.

I led him to my room and turned on a lamp, but Alfonso shook his head. "Too much light," he said. "You have a cloth you can put over the lamp to dim it?"

I threw a red T-shirt over the lamp. Alfonso smiled, and then we both stripped out of our clothes. I kind of wanted him to take mine off for me, but I thought it best just to follow his lead. When we were both naked, he pushed me onto the bed and squatted between my legs. Without another word, he took my penis in his mouth. I could feel his huge organ bumping against my legs as he moved up and down.

I definitely wanted to go to the Celestial Kingdom.

But could I get there if I went through with this?

I wasn't sure a Celestial Kingdom without a man would still be heaven.

After a few glorious minutes, Alfonso turned me over and began massaging my behind. This was really going to happen! I hoped I'd cleaned myself well enough earlier. I heard Alfonso unzipping his bag and heard the sound of latex being stretched. Good. I sure didn't want to catch anything. If I had to go to the doctor, my parents would know.

"Feel this," Alfonso ordered, thrusting some kind of rubber tube into my hand.

"What is it?"

"It's a dildo," he replied. "I'm going to lube it up and slide it into you."

I frowned. "I was kind of hoping for the real thing," I said.

Alfonso laughed. "Oh, you're going to be getting the real thing. It's just that I'm kind of big. We'll need to open you up and relax you before you can take me."

"Okay." Really, I wasn't going to say no to anything he said, was I?

"Let me get this all lubed up." I heard him rubbing something on the dildo. I wished I could lie on my back again while he did this. I wanted to see him, especially when he entered me himself.

I felt something pressing up against my hole, and then suddenly, there was a searing pain. I cried out.

"It's better to shove it all the way in right at the start," he said. "It's like stepping into cold water. Get the pain over with so you can start to enjoy yourself sooner."

"Unh. Okay. Unh. Damn." I could feel myself sweating and tried to relax my sphincter.

"Let me give you a minute," said Alfonso. "I'll be right back."

I heard him step into the bathroom down the hall. After a minute or two, the pain subsided somewhat, and I just wanted him back. I heard the bathroom door open, but Alfonso didn't return. My sphincter clenched again when I heard the front door open.

What the heck?

The neighborhood was so quiet at this hour that I could hear Alfonso starting his car. Had he been upset when I cried out? Decided I was too big a baby to have sex with? I turned over and pulled the T-shirt off the lamp so I could see better. There was a rubber glove on the bed. And the empty tube of lube.

Maybe the guy had stolen something from the living room. My parents were going to kill me. I'd have to say I invited some friends over for a party and someone had taken the missing item. I decided to pull out the dildo and get dressed so I could check.

Unh. The dildo wasn't coming out very easily. Was it supposed to be this difficult? I tugged some more, but the thing wouldn't budge. Was that pressure from the suction? I remembered watching a scene on TV once of a pile driver.

It wasn't coming out. I felt a sudden chill. What if it was stuck? I'd read a story about a man who put a Coke bottle up his butt and then couldn't get it out. I tugged another moment. Then I looked more closely at the lube and my head felt light. It wasn't lubricant. The tube said "Cement glue."

Alfonso had glued the dildo inside me.

I would have to drive to the edge of town and kill myself. What other choice did I have? I sat on the bed, rocking slowly back and forth, feeling the pressure inside my rectum, realizing my life was over.

I pulled on my clothes, just the rubber scrotum protruding from my ass. Everyone would probably think I'd crapped a load in my pants. I climbed into my car and turned on the ignition. "Oh my heck," I kept mumbling. "Oh my heck. Oh my heck." I drove to the emergency room, feeling every bump in the road quite acutely.

It was a Friday night, so the place was busy. I told the triage nurse what the problem was, and she didn't bat an eye. Was this kind of thing normal? "We'll get a police officer to take the report," she said calmly.

I wasn't sure if the criminal aspect of the case advanced me forward in the line, but I was led into an examining room only twenty minutes later. Yet the nightmare wasn't over. It was only getting worse. "Brother Nelson," I spluttered. The doctor was a member of my family's ward.

"Dr. Nelson tonight," he said with a smile. The smile seemed genuine, though he usually acted as stuck up as I did. At least thirty years old and still unmarried, everyone always gossiped that he didn't think anyone else was good enough for him. "So what brings you here tonight?" he asked.

I explained the situation, my cheeks burning, as he examined the piece of rubber extending from my ass. This must be how women felt every time they went to the gynecologist.

"You're the fourth case in as many weeks," Dr. Nelson said. "Always young victims. Two of the others were eighteen. One was seventeen."

"Oh my heck."

"Two of them were approached in a park, one in a restroom. You're lucky all the creep wanted to do was embarrass you. He could've really hurt you."

"How are you going to get it out without ripping my intestines apart?"

"It won't be easy," the doctor admitted. "We'll have to sedate you and go in a couple of millimeters at a time. It's going to take a while. But I expect most of the glue ended up near your anus." He called in a nurse, gave her some instructions, and then turned back to me. "We'll have the police come take your statement when we're done."

I nodded.

A few minutes later, they started an IV, and within seconds, I felt wonderfully calm and relaxed. They positioned me so that my ass was sticking way up in the air, and I felt someone fiddling around with my butthole. I didn't care anymore. I closed my eyes and thought about how cute Dr. Nelson was. Too bad there weren't any other gay Mormons in Bakersfield.

When I woke up sometime later, my ass was burning. "We'll give you some pain meds shortly," Dr. Nelson assured me, "but we wanted to wait until you'd spoken to the police first. I'll be back when you're done." He ushered two officers into the room and then left to take care of his next patient. I told them everything I could remember about Alfonso's car and gave the officers the best description of his face, body, and clothes that I could.

"Come to the station tomorrow, and we'll have a sketch artist work with you."

"I'm eighteen," I said. "You won't tell my parents about this, will you?"

"We're known for our discretion."

Not according to any TV show I'd ever seen. But then, there wasn't much I could do about it.

The officers left, a nurse came in to give me something for the pain, and I rested several minutes until Dr. Nelson came back.

"We'll let you stay a few more hours until enough of this has worn off that you can drive home. It'll be even better if you can get a friend to pick you up. We'll give you a prescription you can fill for the coming week. You're going to need to eat soft foods for the next several days."

"You won't tell the bishop, will you?" I asked. It was one thing to be mortified having my parents hear what had happened, but it was quite another to face church discipline.

"You know, Roderick, I only go to church so I can keep my temple recommend. My younger brothers and sisters are still getting married in the temple, and I don't want to miss that. I have one sister who's still single, but I'm thinking maybe it's time I start concentrating on my own relationships for a change."

Did he not learn in med school that patients weren't interested in the personal problems of their doctors? After all I'd just been through, he was talking about the temple?

"Okay." Maybe he was telling me this to convince me he wouldn't blab. Doctors weren't supposed to blab, anyway, but I'd found that Mormonism usually trumped confidentiality laws.

"So how about we go see a movie next Saturday?"

"What?"

"You won't be my patient after today. It's okay."

"Yes, but…I mean…"

"It'll be too soon for sex," Dr. Nelson went on. "At least the anal kind. But you've always struck me as a smart young man. And now that you're eighteen, and now that I know we play for the same team…"

"My parents will have a cow."

Dr. Nelson shrugged. "Perhaps. But I can help you with tuition if it comes to that. Even if we don't end up in a relationship."

It might have been the meds, but I felt a deep and peaceful warmth, like being hugged from the inside. I could hardly wait till I had a piece of Dr. Nelson inside me as well.

Any orifice would do.

It suddenly occurred to me that it must have been Heavenly Father who'd arranged the entire evening in the first place, to help me meet the man who would take me to the Celestial Kingdom. "The Spirit of God Like a Fire is Burning," I began singing softly.

Dr. Nelson laughed. "Get some rest. I'll try to check in again before you leave." He shook my hand, and I sighed contentedly. I would eat the softest foods I could find this coming week so I'd be ready for a real penis as soon as possible.

I smiled as I watched Dr. Nelson walk out of the room. I lay on the bed in silence, my ass throbbing, and closed my eyes, seeing Alfonso's face clear as day. He'd done me a favor, and I wanted to thank him personally.

I couldn't wait to drive to the police station in the morning.

Becoming Lactose Intolerant

"I think you should change, Natalie," I said. "We're not going to church. The memorial is going to be casual. Dressy casual but casual."

Natalie frowned. "But Adam, it doesn't feel right. I want to show my respect."

"We'll show respect by not dressing like Mormons for a non-Mormon service."

"It's still Salt Lake," she said. "Even if Dustin was excommunicated thirty years ago. His friends need to respect us, too."

"Honey, you look beautiful in those black pants of yours and that red silk shirt."

Natalie wrinkled her nose for a moment but then nodded. "I do like that red shirt," she admitted. "But you're really going to wear that purple one?"

"Purple was Dustin's favorite color."

Natalie shook her head. "Gay people," she said. "What are you gonna do?"

"We'll only stay fifteen or twenty minutes."

Soon we were on our way to the Avenues to the home Dustin had shared for twenty-eight years with Reynaldo. I had to admit I was a little nervous. Not just because I'd only visited my uncle once while he was in the hospital, but because I knew attending the service would force me to think about Ben, something I tried to blot out of my mind whenever I could. Which never amounted to more than a few minutes.

My son had been killed when he fell down some stairs while on his mission to Norway. That had been almost a year ago, and not a single day had passed since that I didn't think about him. The worst part was what his mission president told me a few days after shipping our son's body home.

"I think I should inform you," he said over the phone, "that Elder Marshall had confided to me he'd lost his testimony."

"Excuse me?" I replied, not sure I'd heard correctly.

"I just wanted you to be aware," the mission president went on. "I didn't want you to spend the rest of your lives thinking you were going to be with him again in the next life, and then get to Judgment Day and find out you'll never see him again."

My boy had fallen away? "Uh, thank you, President Dorsey. Th-that was very thoughtful of you." Oh, Ben! I felt my heart dying all over again as I'd hung up the phone.

I never told Natalie about the phone call, but I did talk to Bishop Whitford the following Sunday. I wanted to know what I could or couldn't expect in heaven. "We really don't know the details," he replied. "What's important is to obey all the commandments, read your scriptures, pay your tithing, fulfill your callings, to live your life the way you're supposed to. Heavenly Father will take care of the rest."

"But Bishop, we're the One True Church. Don't we have any better answers than that?"

"Brother Marshall, the answers are most definitely there. The Lord just doesn't want us to know everything yet. We're not supposed to delve into the mysteries."

In the months since, I'd tried to study the gospel more fully, reading another Church book every week. I'd spent most of my life until then just going with the flow, doing what I was told, never questioning. For the longest time, that had worked perfectly well. Until it didn't.

"There's the house," said Natalie. "There sure aren't many places to park on this street."

"So we'll walk," I said. "It's a lovely spring day. The sun is bright, and there's a gentle breeze."

"It's going to mess up my hair."

"Dustin won't mind." He'd been bald the last ten years.

Dustin was my mother's brother. He'd become sexually active with other men shortly after returning from his mission and been excommunicated. Most of the family cut him off, but I'd always liked him, so I kept in touch occasionally during high school, then more often on my mission, and then less often while I pursued my degree and my wife.

There was a long period when the kids were young when I only contacted him once a year, on Christmas. But I never gave up on him altogether. Dustin sometimes seemed distant himself, but then, who could blame him? He had his own life to live, too.

After I parked the car, Natalie and I walked up the street to the old Victorian mansion where Dustin and Reynaldo lived. Or Reynaldo, anyway. What did they need so much space for, I wondered? They never had kids. Not even foster children.

But then maybe it was safer not to have kids.

Natalie grabbed my hand as we started up the path to the front door. We'd been here just once before, for a dinner celebrating the couple's twenty-fifth anniversary. Only ten people attended that event, and I was never clear exactly why Natalie and I were invited, given how ethereal our relationship to Dustin was. We were the only Mormons there as far as I could tell, and boy, did we hear from the rest of the family about "condoning" their "filthy lifestyle."

I knocked on the door and then, hearing lots of noise from inside the house, pushed it open. The living room was filled with people of all ages, though the majority seemed to be older. Most of them looked decidedly gay or lesbian, but some of the others looked normal enough. Probably straight co-workers or something. Maybe they were neighbors.

"Adam. Natalie." Reynaldo came over and gave us each a hug. "Thank you so much for coming. I know Dustin would have been pleased." He handed both of us two blank name tags and a purple Sharpie. "Write your name on one and how you know Dustin on the other." We did so, Natalie looking uncomfortable as she wrote, "Met Dustin through my husband," as if she wasn't sure that was specific enough, or if it disqualified her in some way.

I wrote, "Dustin was my favorite uncle when I was a kid." Reynaldo smiled when I plastered that one on my shirt next to my name. Then he motioned to a table where there were lots of hors d'oeurves. Natalie smiled and headed for the cheese tray. My stomach hurt just thinking about it.

I moved out of the main traffic path and looked about. All I saw were unfamiliar faces. Two effeminate men oohing and ahhing over the festive clothing each was wearing. A woman with a buzz haircut in work clothes, complete with work boots, laughing with another woman, who looked normal. A young man who could barely be twenty, wearing a tight T-shirt and tight pants, following Reynaldo through the room.

I wondered if he was a gold digger. And then I spotted Lorraine, my mother's younger sister, who was a year older than Dustin. I squeezed my way through the crowd. "Aunt Lorraine," I said. "How are you?"

"Missing my little brother," she said with a sigh. "I sure wish more of the family had shown up. Isn't death the one time we can be there for one another? We should mourn with those who mourn." She pointed to the table where Natalie was inserting a toothpick into a meatball. "I brought some funeral potatoes."

We talked about her health, her husband, her kids and grandkids, moving past the crowd and out the back door. I gasped in surprise when I saw Dustin standing in the garden. Oh my goodness. Had they faked his death? Or had he been resurrected? A gay man?

Then I realized the figure was a life-sized cardboard cutout. Dustin in a purple shirt grinning at us all. People stood next to it and had their pictures taken. One last photo with their friend.

"And how are you dealing with Ben's death?" Lorraine asked. She saw the expression on my face and added calmly, "I know perfectly well you're thinking about him today. There's no reason not to be honest about it."

I sighed now, too. "I don't know, Aunt Lorraine. Do you think he's in Spirit Prison?" I bit my lip. I'd never told anyone else about Ben's weakness at the end. "Do you think he's in Paradise? Do you think they're harder on him up there because he came from a good family and should know better not to sin? Do you think—"

"Haven't you gotten any answers in the temple, dear?"

A sixty-year-old man got down on his knees beside the cardboard cutout and pretended to be praying to Dustin while someone took a picture of him. So inappropriate.

"I..."

"I found the temple quite comforting when your grandmother died."

"What answers did you get?" I asked, trying to keep the jealousy out of my voice.

Aunt Lorraine shrugged. "I got the answer that everything would be all right."

I closed my eyes and took a deep breath. "But that's a non answer," I said. "You still don't know anything real." I'd even spoken with one of the General Authorities when I ran into him at City Creek one day. He'd told me basically the same thing. But if an apostle didn't know what waited for us on the Other Side...

"Oh, Adam, when you get to be my age, you understand that there isn't an answer for everything."

"There should be, Lorraine," I said. "There should be."

A woman about thirty-five came out of the house, trailed by two kids about twelve and thirteen. One of the kids was eating a cupcake. The woman's neckline was a bit low, and I could see the top edge of her garments showing through. How in the world did Dustin know her?

Aunt Lorraine put her hand on my arm. "It's milk before meat, sweetie. Line upon line, precept on precept." I didn't say anything, and she continued. "Being LDS is kind of like being a spy. We get everything on a need-to-know basis."

I need to know, I thought.

Natalie joined us and the conversation shifted to something about Relief Society. I left the two of them alone to talk and went back inside to the food table, spreading some chicken salad on a few Ritz crackers.

Ben had loved chicken salad.

Why in the world had he started doubting? We'd raised him so well. He'd excelled in Seminary. Given great talks in church. Become an Eagle Scout, back when that mattered.

Was it possible he'd repent in Spirit Prison and still be able to live with us in the Celestial Kingdom? He was just a kid, after all. It wasn't fair to condemn him before he'd had a chance to really live. Lots of people made mistakes in their youth but came back around given time.

Why hadn't Heavenly Father given him time?

I saw a couple of older women scooping some quinoa and spinach salad onto their plates. I wished my mom had come to the memorial service. But she hadn't spoken to her brother in years. Felt it was pointless. Why waste energy on a relationship that would only last twenty or thirty or even forty more years? You only needed to bother with those you might spend eternity with. Dustin had no chance of making it to the highest degree of heaven.

I wondered why we didn't associate with people of all levels, anyway, as a kind of insurance. It wouldn't hurt to have some ready-made friends available if we ended up in a lower world.

Could I abdicate my godhood and join Ben in the Telestial Kingdom? There was no answer in *Answers to Gospel Questions*.

I wandered back outside, looking for Natalie. We'd made our appearance. We should probably leave now. I didn't see her, but I noticed a table set up in the yard with several photo albums. I walked over and opened one, seeing photos of Dustin teaching Latino kids to read. Or maybe he was teaching them English. It was hard to tell exactly what was going on. Other pictures showed my uncle building the frame for a wall along with a group of other people.

It looked like a Habitat for Humanity project. A few pages later, there was a picture of Dustin drinking coffee at a cafe, presumably in Paris. After I finished the album, I moved on to the next one, trading with the woman beside me. I could see the border of her garments making a ridge under her blouse.

Another Mormon. In the new album, there were more pictures of Dustin with various friends, drinking alcohol, holding a protest sign proclaiming, "Joseph Smith had 32 wives. I only want 1 husband." Such poor taste. There were photos of Dustin crossing a swinging bridge, of Dustin standing in Times Square.

Other than my two years in Portugal, I'd never traveled anywhere interesting. I'd never even been to Yellowstone, and that wasn't very far away.

Natalie and I had planned to go to Norway to pick Ben up at the end of his mission.

I didn't even know most of this stuff about my uncle. The few times a year I spoke with him, he usually talked about books he was reading or a movie he'd just seen. Many of those movies had been rated R, so I could never watch them myself and as a result found the discussions rather meaningless. We had so little in common. And yet I still kept calling. And he kept sending Christmas cards.

But why? None of that had brought us particularly close in this life, and like my mother said, we were unlikely to be together on the Other Side. So why did I bother?

Was it to feel a tiny sense of liberation by proxy?

"Okay, everyone." Reynaldo poked his head out the back door. "It's time for everyone to come in and pick out one of Dustin's books."

I wasn't sure what that was all about but squeezed back into the house, the twenty or so people outside filling in the tight gaps between the twenty or thirty other guests already inside. Thank goodness it was a big house. I found Natalie talking to Lorraine and navigated my way over to them, trying not to knock the cups out of people's hands along the way. Natalie handed me a piece of peanut butter fudge.

"The books on these shelves all belonged to Dustin," Reynaldo said. "I want you each to pick out one book. Over here are nameplates with Dustin's name on them. Take one and paste it into the book you've chosen. Then in this log..." He pointed. "...write down your name and which book you took and why. Plus write a short memory about Dustin."

This part of the service took another half hour. So much for getting out quickly. I picked a book about the National Tile Museum in Lisbon. But I didn't know what memory to write down in the log. I was afraid to hold up the line, so I finally wrote the only thing I could think of. "Dustin came to my son's funeral and held me while I cried."

"Why didn't I make more time for him as I grew older?" I asked. Natalie was scribbling in the log beside me. She wrote, "Dustin was always well dressed." What might I have learned if I'd just spent a little more time with him?

"Who knows?" she said. "Maybe you were trying not to lose the Spirit. You wouldn't have been a good father if you lost the Spirit."

Did I really avoid Dustin just because he loved another man?

"I want to see him again," I said. "I want to be with him again." I was talking about Ben.

Natalie shook her head. "He's gone forever now."

Oh, Ben. But I decided to answer as I'd been talking about my uncle all along. "I can do his work in the temple."

"He had his chance. He chose not to follow what he knew to be true."

I blinked my eyes dry.

I left Natalie holding her book, a cookbook featuring French recipes, and headed back to the table covered with food. I looked longingly at the sliced Havarti next to a cake of brie. Mormons couldn't get drunk, but we could overeat. And that cheese looked comforting.

I'd tried to comfort Natalie, but after the first few months, she seemed fine, content to wait a few years before being reunited with our son once more.

I didn't understand.

I looked at the cheese plate again, irritated I couldn't eat dairy anymore. I'd read somewhere that almost everyone developed digestive issues associated with milk as they aged. The condition progressed more rapidly in those who didn't consume much dairy to begin with. But I drank milk every day. Or used to, anyway. Why was I having trouble? It wasn't fair.

Ben was just a kid. Heavenly Father was mean.

I wanted to know why!

I turned around and came face to face with Bishop Whitford. "Good afternoon, Adam."

"Bishop! What are you doing here?"

"Your mother mentioned that her brother had passed." He reached over and grabbed the Havarti I'd ignored. "She was afraid she wouldn't be worthy to go to the temple if she attended the memorial. I assured her she would, but she was adamant. I came so I could tell her all about it." He took a bite of the cheese. "She didn't tell me you'd be here."

"She doesn't know," I said.

"It's quite a nice turnout, I see." He surveyed the room.

"Bishop," I said, "why does the Church give us so little information about what happens after death? We used to talk about becoming gods, but even that doctrine was always pretty fuzzy."

"The Lord doesn't want to distract us. Our job is to focus on living a good life."

"But why? It's like running down a football field without even knowing if there's an end zone ahead. How can we play the game right if we don't know the whole setup?"

Bishop Whitford laughed. "We see through a glass darkly."

I wanted to shake him. "That's exactly my point!" I could hear my voice rising and took a moment to calm down. "I want answers. We're supposed to know more than other religions. Why doesn't the Church teach us the hard stuff? We should know what we're supposed to be getting."

"Brother Marshall," the bishop said softly, "I can see you're agitated. Why don't you come to my office for a chat after Sacrament this Sunday?"

I looked him in the eyes. There was kindness in them. "Are you going to be able to answer any of my questions in your office?"

Bishop Whitford tried to keep looking back into my own eyes, but he faltered and turned back toward the cheese plate. "The Lord can't give the answers to only some of us," he said. "Word would get out. And most people aren't ready for meat. So we have to be satisfied with milk."

Over the next few seconds, I felt a tremendous surge of rage. I felt my head might explode, that my eyeballs would pop out of their sockets. And then, just as suddenly, the rage vanished and was replaced with an eerie calm. "I think I'm becoming lactose intolerant," I said.

The bishop frowned and I walked away. I saw Reynaldo talking with two men. They looked almost normal. The only thing that gave the two guys away was that they were dressed a little too neatly. Reynaldo didn't seem particularly sad or troubled today, but then, Dustin had been ill for the last four months. He'd hardly been taken by surprise.

Still, I suspected what he must really be feeling, how hard it had to be keeping up a front. I joined him and the other two men, nodding slightly when Reynaldo looked over at me to see if I was going to join in.

When the men left a few minutes later, I looked at Dustin's husband and saw the change on his face as he looked back. I reached forward and put my arms around him. He put his arms around me as well.

And I held him for the longest time while we cried.

Koriwhoredoms

"Marsha, something's wrong." I leaned my head toward the passenger side window and listened. I could hear an odd noise, kind of a rushing sound. "I think you have a flat."

"Really?" she replied. "I don't feel anything, Arlene."

"You'd better pull over before we get on the freeway."

Marsha moved onto the narrow shoulder, brushing against some weeds. We were on a desolate stretch of East Marginal Way in south Seattle, industrial where there were buildings, but there weren't many buildings. A perfect place for two stranded women to be raped, I thought. Marsha walked around to the front of the car, looked down at the right front tire, and nodded her head wearily. Then she came back and climbed behind the wheel. "Do we have a spare?" I asked.

"That one *is* the spare," Marsha replied. "The original tire had a flat months ago, and we couldn't afford to buy a new one."

"You think we can get this one patched?"

Marsha shook her head. "It's almost bald. But I still have the other tire back at the house. I'll bring that one to Goodyear and see if they can repair it." She opened her door and stepped outside again.

"I'd better call my boss." I pulled out my cell phone and called Barry, waking him up. I explained I'd be a little late and that he'd have to open the store this morning, but that I was on my way. Marsha always drove me to work in White Center on Sundays because I had to be at the video store for 7:20, and it took three buses over ninety minutes to get there on public transportation.

I'd had to sell my car months ago. Marsha wasn't a morning person, so I hated waking her up on her one day off, but she insisted, and it always gave us a chance to talk about our upcoming week.

Those conversations, unfortunately, had become more and more grim as the months passed.

I fought my way through the weeds, joined Marsha on the shoulder, and we started walking back the way we'd come. The air was chilly, and a light, misting rain was falling. I watched as Marsha hugged herself against the cold. I wanted to hold her hand but didn't dare in this neighborhood.

It was my fault we didn't have a spare tire. It was my fault we were ten days late with the electric bill. It was my fault we were eating Vienna sausages from Grocery Outlet for dinner.

Finances had become increasingly stressful the past couple of years since I'd been fired from my job as an accountant. I'd made an honest but serious mistake in my work, getting the company in trouble. I was lucky I wasn't in jail. I'd applied for over thirty other accounting jobs since but had never even been granted an interview. It was clear I was on some kind of blacklist.

I supposed I could have kept applying for more accounting positions until I found one that might take a chance on me, but the truth was I'd grown to hate the job. Leaving Seattle to find work elsewhere was out of the question, unfortunately. Neither of us wanted to move away from our kids and grandkids, even if they hadn't spoken to us in eight years, not since Marsha and I moved in together.

Scientologists weren't the only people who "disconnected" from apostate members. Mormons were good at it, too.

After about five minutes, we reached the road heading back toward Rainier Beach, and Marsha leaned over to kiss me. I noticed a man in a hooded jacket on the other side of the street and hesitated. When Marsha frowned, I completed the kiss. "We'll get through this," I said.

She nodded unconvincingly and started into the crosswalk. I watched long enough to make sure the man didn't turn to follow her. Then I kept walking. I probably had two miles or more to reach the bridge leading to South Park. I could see a bus stop for the 124 on the other side of the street, but the bus surely wouldn't run often on a Sunday morning.

It would be just as quick to walk, and walking would help me deal with the morning's tension. But fifteen minutes later, I was just coming up on Randy's diner, and I knew that was still another two full miles from my destination.

The "d" on Randy's was broken, reading "Ranay's."

I walked on for a few more minutes and then went ahead and crossed over to the bus stop. I'd been walking twenty minutes. The bus would surely be by soon.

Three minutes later, I swiped my Orca card against the reader and sat up front so I could best see when I reached my stop. This wasn't my usual bus route, my normal three buses taking me on a much more circuitous path. We passed the Museum of Flight and half a dozen other Boeing buildings.

I pulled the cord a moment later, crossed back over Marginal Way, and waited at another bus stop for the 60, my regular bus, the last of the three I took. It stopped by a mere seven minutes later, a miracle on a Sunday, and soon I was in White Center.

"A miracle," I said in disgust.

I didn't believe in miracles anymore. I'd believed back when I met Marsha, back when we both worked in Young Women. I was the Beehive instructor and she taught the Laurels. Finding love for the first time in my late forties seemed like a gift from God. I could understand well enough why Norton no longer spoke to me. But it hurt that my kids had turned on me, too.

I stopped at the gas station on the corner of 15th and SW Roxbury and bought a lottery ticket. The Asian man running the store was watching a movie on his phone and took a couple of minutes before waiting on me. I was irritated, but I was already late, and I wanted my ticket. Then I walked on to 16th.

The last two blocks of my commute were always frightening, no matter the time of day. A Hispanic man had been killed back at the bus stop just two days ago while waiting for the 60, in the middle of the day. This stretch of White Center housed a smoke shop, a pot shop, a pizza parlor, a boxing ring, a pawn shop, a billiard hall, a tattoo parlor, two massage parlors—why were so many seedy businesses called parlors?—a few bars, and a payday loan place.

I wasn't sure why no one had ever thought of a better description than "place." It was so generic. Maybe we should call it a payday loan parlor. An Asian market was opening up next to a closed taqueria. Few people were out on the streets this time of the day, but I passed a homeless man sleeping in the doorway of a boarded up bakery. A moment later, I saw a scuzzy-looking white man approaching from the block ahead.

Even though I wasn't at a corner, I crossed the street to continue toward the store. The man crossed the street as well.

What was I going to do? I had two cans of V8 in my bag, making it heavy enough to use as a weapon. The man continued walking toward me. Should I cross back to the other side of the street again? Should I duck into a bar?

I wondered if Marsha was okay. She was in such a deserted area.

The man passed me and kept walking. I let out a deep breath and hurried the rest of the way to the store, arriving just after 8:00. The "Open" sign was still off, and the front door was locked. Had Barry fallen back asleep after I called? I unlocked the door but didn't hear the warning beep from the alarm. Pushing my way in, I saw Barry at the cash register. He was a black man a few years younger than I was.

"Arlene!" he said. "I'm so glad you made it!"

I smiled and put my bag down in the tiny office space behind the counter.

"I've run the reports but haven't had a chance to empty the trash cans in the arcade or the theater. Here, let me hand the register over to you."

I started counting my till while Barry finished sorting through some papers. Once I verified the drawer had $200, I counted the safe. The max it ever held was $1000 but often there was less. This morning, there were only two bundles of ones and one bundle of fives, plus a hundred dollars in coin and loose bills. $400. "We'll need some cash before you go," I said.

"Then it's just as well I came early. I don't want to miss the game later." He grabbed the key to the little alley behind the arcade and went in to pull out whatever bills had been deposited the day before.

I grabbed a trash bag, put on a rubber glove, and started emptying the trash cans in the booths. Most of them were filled with used paper towels. A few of the towels had bits of feces stuck to them, but the majority were just soaked in cum. In one trash can, they were soaked with urine. Some receptacles had empty condom wrappers and used condoms. "Oh!" I said at one point.

Lying on top of the contaminated paper towels was a five dollar bill. Someone must have dropped it accidentally the day before. I usually found a few bills every month, mostly ones, on the floor of the booths. I picked up the five dollar bill and put it in my pocket.

I quickly made a run through the theater as well. Here, I discovered a used cucumber on one of the sofas. I threw the filthy thing in the trash and then grabbed some disinfectant and a paper towel to clean the sofa. Before long, both Barry and I were back at the counter. He added a few more bundles of fives and ones to the safe, and I checked in a DVD that our first customer of the day brought back. *My Stepdaughter Likes My Uncut Dick.*

"Good news," Barry said, locking up the safe. "For you, anyway."

"Yes?"

"Come January, the minimum wage goes up. It'll be hard on me, but I have to do it."

I stared at him. Was my boss expecting me to commiserate? I only worked three days a week as it was because Barry refused to hire people full time, so he could avoid giving his employees health insurance, sick leave, or vacation. And now he was bitching about having to pay us minimum wage? "I'll take my twenty cents, thank you," I wanted to say but just smiled at him instead.

Oh, how the mighty have fallen, I thought. I'd once been first counselor in the Relief Society.

Soon Barry was gone, and I was back to my usual Sunday morning routine. Only one or two customers came in per hour the first few hours, so I normally just relaxed and listened to music, making sure to keep the baseball bat behind the counter handy in case some creep tried to drag me in back. Thanksgiving wasn't for four more days, but already my two favorite light rock stations were only playing Christmas songs. I shrugged, set the dial on 101.5, and called Marsha. She picked up on the third ring.

"How're you doing?" I asked.

"Almost home," she replied.

Good grief. It was 8:45. But there were a lot of hills between Marginal Way and our house in Rainier Beach. "How are you going to get the tire to Goodyear?"

"I'll borrow Evelyn's truck." Evelyn and Gail lived three blocks from us. We were all part of a lesbian book club that met once a month. Evelyn, I remembered, had made a strong impression on me when I first met her four years ago. She'd gone on and on about how the only way to fly to Europe was on Emirates because their first class wasn't just a large, comfy seat but an entire cabin complete with bed. Even four years ago, when I'd still made good money, that had struck me as overly privileged.

Evelyn liked Marsha more than she liked me.

"Well, good luck," I said. "Call me when you find out if they can patch the other tire."

I sat down and looked out over the store, surveying the vibrators and lingerie while Wham! sang "Last Christmas." I didn't know what we were going to do if Marsha couldn't repair that tire. She was self-employed as a housekeeper and carried her own supplies to the different houses she cleaned.

Her income would be cut off without the car, and she didn't work enough jobs to bring home that much as it was. The mortgage was due tomorrow, and we were still a hundred dollars short. Marsha had assured me she could get the money to me by morning.

Maybe someone would drop a hundred dollar bill in the trash today.

I listened to "Rockin' Around the Christmas Tree" and "Have a Holly Jolly Christmas." A customer came in, went into the arcade, and came out a moment later because there was no one else in there to play with. "Anybody in the theater?" he asked.

"Not yet, but you can go in and prime the pump." Someone had to go in first so that other men would follow.

The customer frowned and walked out the door. A half hour later, an older white man came in and checked out *Squirt on My*

Face. As much as I tried to act liberated after leaving the Church, I still felt that a great deal of the pornography out there was pretty degenerate. Straight porn was the worst, almost always demonstrating a power dynamic where the woman was the object.

In gay porn, both men were more or less equal. Even then, gay porn made by straight directors mirrored a straight porn hierarchy more than gay porn made by gay men. Lesbian porn was really directed at straight men rather than women, so it often felt unsatisfying as well.

The radio blasted out "Joy to the World" and "God Rest Ye Merry Gentlemen."

The phone rang. The Caller ID said "Private Number," so I didn't pick up. Private Number was a crank caller who called almost every day. I'd long since learned not to answer. A white man came in and bought a bottle of Rush. Another white man came in, handed me a twenty, and asked for it all back in ones. I hated going through so many bills on just one customer. It meant going to the safe an extra time during my shift.

I was almost out of ones already. The guy went into booth number eleven, one with glory holes on each side. We referred to these booths as those which had been "vandalized" since we couldn't legally allow the holes. Only half our booths had them.

The phone rang again. The Caller ID showed Marsha's number. "How'd it go?" I asked.

"They were able to fix the hole for $15," she said.

"What a relief."

"I'm headed back to the car now. I hope it doesn't get towed before I get there."

"Can Evelyn help you change the tire?"

"I can change a tire by myself."

"Give me a call when you get home."

"Love you."

To be honest, I'd been surprised to discover that marriage to someone I really wanted to be with was almost as challenging as the marriage to my husband had been. For some reason, I'd expected something different. Marsha didn't even like sex that much. Sometimes, I wished I could go into the arcade after work and take some man's penis through the partition.

I'd never liked intercourse very much, but I'd kind of enjoyed oral sex. But Marsha and I were monogamous. Her husband had cheated on her during their marriage, and she'd never been able to forgive him, even after his blessings had been restored when he was rebaptized.

Marsha and I had never gone to bed together until after we'd left our husbands.

I listened to Karen Carpenter sing "There's No Place Like Home for the Holidays." Nat King Cole followed up with "Chestnuts Roasting on an Open Fire."

A Latino with lipodystrophy walked into the store, and I sighed. "Jorge," I said, "the boss says you can't come in here anymore."

He frowned. "Why not?"

"Some of the other customers are afraid you have HIV." It was a ridiculous reason to kick him out. I knew of at least two other regulars who had HIV, plus another who told me he had herpes. Men having anonymous sex with strangers needed to expect that every sexual encounter carried risks and take appropriate precautions to protect themselves each and every time.

Jorge's face fell, and I felt the way I had when the bishop quizzed me at fifteen about masturbation. Jorge had told me a few weeks ago about the custody battle he was fighting for his five-year-old son. The child's mother used drugs but wouldn't give the boy up. "She knew I was bisexual before we had the baby," he told me, "but now she's using that against me."

"There are a couple of other arcades you can go to," I said. "There's one in Des Moines and another in Tukwila."

He shook his head. "They're too far."

"I'm really sorry, Jorge."

He nodded glumly and walked out of the store. A moment later, the guy with herpes came in and went straight to the arcade. I checked on the monitor to make sure he put a dollar in the machine since he was one of our regulars who often "forgot."

I listened to "What Child Is This?" and "Feliz Navidad."

I'd served a mission to Guatemala and Marsha had served in Mexico, so we often spoke Spanish to each other. But our Spanish was decades old, and we were always afraid the Hispanic people around us were laughing at our mistakes. Speaking our mission language together made us feel we were still a little Mormon, however, even if no other Mormons would talk to us anymore. Why we cared, I didn't know.

I needed to pee, and since there was no one out front right then looking at the many items which could be easily shoplifted, I hurried to the bathroom. Inside, I looked down at the toilet and groaned. Someone had dumped half a dozen paper towels into the bowl.

I supposed I was lucky the customer hadn't flushed, as that would have clogged the toilet, but I was still irritated. It didn't look like the paper towels had any feces on them, though, so I reached into the toilet, scooped out the wet paper, and tossed it in the trash can. Then I washed my hands, pulled a toilet seat cover from the dispenser, and sat down.

"Do You Hear What I Hear?" I heard the loudspeaker singing. I also heard the back door open, so I hurried up, flushed, and headed back to the register. An Asian man was waiting to ask for change. He handed me a ten dollar bill. I handed him back a five and five ones. Then I bought another bundle of ones from the safe.

Not long after, the phone rang, and I picked up. "Everything good, Marsha?" I asked.

"I've got the tire in place," she said, "but I left the emergency lights on, and now the battery is dead. I'll need to take it to the store and see if it can be salvaged."

"Oh, Marsha."

"I'll call you when I find out."

A voice in the back of my head told me Heavenly Father was punishing us for leaving the Church. Yet another voice told me the first voice was the whispering of the Holy Ghost. But who was the second voice?

A white man came in and bought a ticket to the theater, informing me a guy he'd met online was due to meet him here. I didn't know why he felt I needed to know this. But ten minutes later when another man asked for a ticket, I told him his date was inside waiting for him. He blushed.

Really?

Several more guys went into the arcade over the next half hour. I had to go in back twice to remind people to keep money in the machine. I ate a peanut butter cracker I'd brought with me and sipped some of my V8. I listened as Eartha Kitt sang "Santa Baby" and then as Judy Garland crooned "Have Yourself a Merry Little Christmas." I felt like Margaret O'Brien.

The front door chime sounded, and I looked up to see a homeless man who'd come in several times before. I'd kicked him out last time because on his visit before that, he'd smelled so bad I used almost an entire can of air freshener to make the arcade habitable again. "I'm going to have to ask you to leave," I said.

"But I took a shower last night!" he said. "I washed my clothes!"

I had in fact told him that he needed to go to one of the hygiene centers located about the city before I would let him in again. Since his clothes did look clean today, and I couldn't smell him from across the counter, I nodded and waved him on in to the arcade. Ten minutes later when I made my rounds to clean up after some other guys who had left, I smelled him the instant I walked back there.

Goddammit. And on the monitor, I saw that he'd purchased over twenty minutes of booth time. I couldn't very well kick him out after he'd paid. I watched on the video feed as other men saw the light above his door and eagerly went into the adjacent booth, only to come out seconds later when they realized what was on the other side of the wall. Homeless people needed sex, too, but the guy *really* should have gone to a hygiene center first.

The phone rang. It was a guy asking if we had dildoes that squirted up one's butt. I told him we just had the regular kind. I suggested two other stores he could call. He thanked me and hung up.

I listened to the Peanuts Christmas theme and to Pachelbel's Canon in D.

I sold three $9.95 DVDs for our sale price of $20. Then I sold a bottle of three Buckram male enhancement pills. I thought again about Norton's dick. Maybe it would've been better to join a fundamentalist sect and still have access to my husband's penis along with the clitorides of my sister wives.

"God of Our Fathers," I hummed softly during a commercial break.

I missed the Church. The more distance I had from those faithful days, the more I realized how fraught with problems almost every aspect of Mormon life was. But at the time, I'd enjoyed it.

I wanted to go to the temple with Marsha. Even if we both had to wear a veil.

A white man came to the counter and checked out three DVDs. One was *Fucking All My Ex-Wives in the Ass*. I was amazed by how many men liked anal. Norton never would have dared ask such a thing of me. He even felt compelled to confess to the bishop whenever I went down on him.

The phone rang again. "Marsha?" I asked.

"I need a new battery," she said. "It's $170."

"Oh my God."

"I'll have to use my line of credit," she said, "and repay it tomorrow with the money I was going to give you. Otherwise, I won't be able to go to work in the morning."

I shook my head wearily. "Call me when you get home."

I sat down and watched a heavy Latino man who was loitering suspiciously near the cock rings. "Can I help you?" I asked.

"No, no, just looking," he said. He hung around another couple of minutes, glancing at me over his shoulder, and then left. Thank God he didn't beep on the way out.

The homeless man finally left, and I went to spray his booth, discovering he'd left a second gift in addition to the odor. Skid marks on his chair. I wiped down the chair and threw the paper towel into the trash. That's when I saw the crumpled five dollar bill on the floor. I picked it up and shoved it in my pocket.

Taking money from a homeless man. Could I sink any lower?

I listened as the radio blared out "We Need a Little Christmas" and "Simply Having a Wonderful Christmas Time."

An elderly white man asked if I would go back in the theater with him. I smiled and showed him my wedding ring. He smiled back and showed me his. I shook my head, and he went into the theater by himself.

I used to teach the Young Women about chastity.

My Patriarchal Blessing said I'd been a valiant spirit in the Pre-Existence.

I sold a small bottle of Swiss Navy silicone lubricant to a black guy heading for the theater. Lots of guys wanted sex without a condom. I buzzed him past the gate.

Barry called to make sure everything was going okay. I told him it was. I got another call from a guy asking if we sold glass pipes. I told him we did. Then I sold a young white man a box of nitrous oxide canisters. They were ten percent off this week.

I wondered how my kids and grandkids were doing.

I also wondered what I was going to buy Marsha for Christmas. So far, all I had was a 500-piece puzzle of a Mexican plaza that I'd bought at the dollar store. But we had to be practical. Maybe I should buy her a can of Lysol for work.

An East African man came in and bought two dildoes. A Filipino who was a regular came in and told me he was suffering a shingles outbreak. I wasn't sure how he managed to feel sexually excited while he was in so much pain, but he went in back to spread the virus. A Latino came to the counter and asked me to recommend the best lubricant. I picked one at random and sold it to him.

The phone rang. "Hi, Arlene." Marsha sounded tired, but then, she'd been running around since 7:00 this morning. "When I got back to the car, I discovered someone had ransacked it."

"Oh, no."

"They stole the jack, of all things."

"Anything else?"

"A bucket of cleaning supplies."

I'd asked Marsha several times not to leave valuables in the car, but she got so tired of carrying everything back and forth to the house. There was nothing to be gained by saying anything now. "Are you home?" I asked.

"Yes."

I looked at my watch. It was 3:15. "I'll be off soon," I said. My shift ended at 4:30. "I found some money in the arcade. How about I stop at the taco truck on my way home and get us some burritos for dinner?"

"That would be great, Arlene. Thank you."

"Take a nap," I said. "And I'll give you a foot rub after we eat."

"See you in a little while, hon."

I noticed she hadn't asked anything about my day. But then, what was there to say? "Some guys came in and had sex." When my life wasn't boring, it was unmentionable. Of course, it wasn't as if Marsha came home with fascinating tales of housecleaning, either. It was hard to feel connected when both our lives were so empty.

We used to talk about Gospel Doctrine class. Jesus healing the sick. The different landscapes and animals we might create once we were gods.

A black man came to the counter and bought a previously viewed DVD for $12.88. *Phat Ass White Girls*. I asked if he needed any lube to go with the movie, and he bought a small bottle of ID Glide. There was a short lull after that, so I took advantage of the opportunity to buy another bundle of fives as I listened to "Do They Know It's Christmas?" and "Walking in a Winter Wonderland."

I missed my childhood Christmases in Salt Lake. But then, I also missed my one Guatemalan Christmas. And I missed my Christmases here in Seattle with Norton and the kids.

I had to find some way to make Marsha feel special this year in the midst of all this mess. Maybe I could find a better job. At least a full-time minimum wage position. I hadn't wanted to be a housekeeper like she was. Cleaning was a part of my former life that no longer excited me. But maybe I should apply at the Marriott anyway. It might be more palatable taking money from a rich Mormon, though I didn't really know why.

I wondered if I could secretly contact one of Marsha's daughters and get her to call or at least send a card. It seemed too risky, though. Her oldest daughter had called Marsha a Korihor, and her youngest had called her a Judas. The middle daughter, I remembered, had called Marsha an Emma, apparently thinking that was a slur because Joseph Smith's first wife hadn't followed Brigham Young out west with the "real" saints.

We would have stayed Latter-day Saints if they'd let us.

I gave out more change, bought another bundle of ones from the safe, and then counted the rest of the safe to get it ready for the night shift. Philip would be coming soon. At least he was always on time. I sold an old white man in his seventies some magazines, sold another white man about my age a bottle of Jungle Juice, and sold a young Middle Eastern man a spider web body stocking. I didn't ask if it was for himself or a female friend. Or a male friend, for that matter.

Marsha still wore her garments. I'd wasted all sorts of money buying her beautiful lingerie to no avail. But at least she didn't make me wear them, too. I had to admit, though, I felt a certain nostalgia every night when I saw her coming to bed.

Maybe we could still be goddesses together.

An Asian man came up to the counter to buy a DVD called *Big Tit MILFs Want Facials*. After he left, I made another round through the arcade. I saw a penny on the floor and debated picking it up but decided against it. I wasn't that desperate, was I?

After I sat back down behind the counter, I gritted my teeth and returned to the arcade to pick up the penny.

Mariah Carey sang, "All I Want for Christmas Is You." Rob Thomas sang "New York Christmas." John Lennon sang, "So This Is Christmas."

It was finally time to start counting my drawer. This was always tricky, trying to count soon enough that I'd be ready to hand over the drawer the instant my relief came but not wanting to count so early that another customer came to do a transaction after I finished and I had to count all over again.

If only all my troubles were so petty.

Soon Philip was there, I printed out my closing paperwork, and I signed out of the computer. I grabbed my bag, wished Philip a good evening, and headed for the taco truck. While I was waiting in line, my cell buzzed. "Hi, Marsha, I'm getting our burritos now."

"I went to take our two coin jars to Safeway to get cash," she said.

"Yes?" I doubted there'd be the hundred dollars we needed.

"The car starts all right, so it's not the new battery, but it's making a funny noise, like something is beating wrong."

I looked up into the cloudy sky, almost dark since it was nearly sundown. I wondered if the guy who'd broken in had tampered with the engine, or if this was just one more bad bit of luck.

"Why, Heavenly Father?" I whispered. "Why?" Then I spoke directly into the phone.

"We'll get through this, Marsha," I said. "We'll get through this."

"I love you, you know."

"I love you, too."

I wondered if it even mattered.

"See you in ninety minutes," I replied. I picked up my burritos and headed for the bus stop, where there was a tiny memorial made out of candles and plastic flowers. Everyone left it alone. A few minutes later, the 60 pulled up, and I climbed aboard. I hoped Thanksgiving this Thursday with Evelyn, Gail, and the rest of book club would go well.

And I hoped we had enough money to make the rolls.

Amen

"Dear Heavenly Father," I began, "please help me do well on this test." I was on my way to the Garfield Community Center in the Central District to take a skills test for a City job as a cashier. "Please help me to—"

Stop it, Ron, I told myself. There's no God. Stop praying for stuff. It's a simple math test. Just take it.

I looked at my watch. The 106 was due any minute. If it had come early, though, I'd have to wait another twenty minutes for the next bus. "Dear Heavenly Father," I prayed, "please help the bus be on time."

Stop it.

The bus was either about to come or it wasn't. Even if there were a God, he could hardly create an extra bus complete with bus driver and passengers. If the bus came on time, great. If not, I'd have to deal with it. I'd left the house with plenty of time to spare.

The sun was hot on this late August afternoon. But we'd had a decent summer here in Seattle, only eight days above 90, most days in the upper 70s to about 80. It could have been worse.

"Thank you, Heavenly Father," I began.

Oh, good grief.

I'd been raised Mormon, taught to "pray always." Even after being excommunicated thirty years ago, I'd kept my belief in God, despite all evidence to the contrary. The last few years, though, I simply found it impossible to believe anymore.

Ah, there was the bus coming over the top of the hill. I breathed a sigh of relief and grabbed my Orca Lift card which let me pay half fare. I'd only been able to find a part-time job the past year and a half after losing my full-time job at the bank, and every month was a struggle to pay the bills, even with Jeremy's help.

I needed that cashier job. It would require constant traveling to a dozen or more locations, some job sites requiring me to board three different buses to get there, but at least the position had benefits.

"Dear Heavenly Father—"

I climbed onto the bus and found a seat.

I'd loved the Mormon idea of eternal progression, taking as long to reach perfection as my personality required. God had always been a benevolent force in my life. The bad things in the world happened because of Satan.

But there sure were a lot of bad things.

What kind of god worth worshipping was weaker than Satan, or gave him a free hand, allowed him to cause so much misery to both humans and animals? And plants and insects, too, for that matter. I'd always accepted that "there must needs be opposition in all things," that misery helped us to "grow," but the absolute degree of suffering that existed was far too great to justify.

I remembered seeing on TV once a clip from a home movie shot by a murderer as he promised a handcuffed couple that he'd torture and kill their baby before killing them, hitchhikers who'd accepted the wrong free ride. The look on their faces was a pitiful combination of both despair and resignation. I was still haunted by it.

What possible "growth" experience could this family need to justify what they were about to endure? And what did it say about a God whose best plan to "help" his children was to allow such horror?

The bus pulled onto Rainier, and I thought about switching to the 7. It would probably be a little faster, but I hated transfers, and I still had one more bus to catch at a minimum. I decided to stick with the 106.

I sure hoped I did okay on this math test. It would be simple arithmetic, after all, and I did have a Biology degree, giving me plenty of practice in both physics and chemistry. I could certainly add up a few figures. But what if my calculator died? What if I hit the wrong button in my arrogance? What if my pencil broke?

"Dear Heavenly Father, please—"

I felt guilty for not finishing my prayers. Wouldn't these half-finished pleas irritate Heavenly Father?

What kind of God would want to be pestered non-stop even by completed petitionary prayers that did nothing but emphasize my selfish needs and desires? I'd heard a rabbi say once that only prayers of praise were appropriate. But what kind of god needed to have his ass kissed every day?

I thought maybe prayers asking God to help others, the poor, the sick, those in war-torn countries, those in prison, might be acceptable, but what kind of God withheld his aid from the needy until some random third person requested he step in?

I saw an East African immigrant in a hijab running for the bus on Martin Luther King. There was no way she was going to make it on time. I wanted to pray for her, but it was pointless. She'd either make it or she wouldn't.

She didn't make it.

Was it my fault?

Oh, Ron.

I'd been fighting the compulsion to pray for six months now. I sometimes went long stretches, five hours or more, without being tempted, but whenever a real "crisis" came along, I found myself reverting to my old habits.

Like when I had to have blood drawn and wanted the phlebotomist to hit the vein right on the first try, or when someone wanted to return an item to the drugstore but didn't have their receipt and I had to satisfy both the customer and the manager.

I needed to do well on this test.

Before long, we were at the Mount Baker Transit Center, and I stepped off the bus and walked over to the sign for the 48, checking the schedule. The bus should be here in just two more minutes. Unless it had come early.

"Dear—"

Deal with it, Ron, I told myself. Deal with it.

If there were a God, he wouldn't want me to depend so heavily on him, must have been annoyed as hell at me all these years. He'd want me to fend for myself, overcome my challenges and make something of my life. He'd want *me* to do that, not him. He would already know what *he* could do.

I still thought of God as a he, comfortable with this bit of patriarchy, despite what that probably said about me.

A young black woman with a baby stroller walked over to the 48 sign as well. And a middle-aged Latino man.

Just the other few people at this same bus stop probably needed more help than I did. Why should God, if there were such a being, want to help *me*? But then, why did this have to be an either/or question? Surely, if God was omnipotent, he could help everyone who needed helping.

I shook my head. One thing was clear—if there were truly a benevolent being out there, it certainly rationed its assistance.

The 48 pulled up a moment later, and I waited for the others to board. Then I found a seat in the first row past Priority Seating so I could still see out the front window and be on the lookout for the community center. I wasn't very familiar with the neighborhood around Garfield.

I'd been five days late with my last mortgage payment, and I was three months—three months!—behind on my Visa bill. If I didn't pass this test, and the subsequent interview, Jeremy and I weren't going to make it. He was a self-employed contractor but only did piddly little jobs that hardly brought home any more money than my part-time minimum wage job. We faced disaster every month, and given that there was in fact no Supreme Being to protect us, our luck wasn't going to hold out forever. I *had* to get this job. It was up to *me*.

We passed the Northwest African American History Museum and kept heading north on 23rd. We passed the Sojourner Truth library and kept going.

I missed Heavenly Father. Even if he wasn't real, I used to *think* he was. I talked to him all the time, not just about my immediate needs but also about my dreams and goals and what things he might want of me. I felt the way now that I had all those years ago when my mother died of leukemia.

But praying wasn't a harmless habit. It shifted responsibility from me to someone else. And it was important—essential—that I take responsibility for myself. *I* needed to fight for a $15 minimum wage. *I* needed to fight against fracking. *I* needed to work to restore voting rights to disenfranchised ex-convicts. It wasn't enough to ask God to "help me" do these things. It was up to me to *do* them.

The glory was supposed to go to God, though, wasn't it? It wasn't right to take credit myself.

There was Garfield High School. The community center couldn't be far away. Yes, there it was. I pulled the cord and made my way to the door.

Stepping off the bus, I looked at my watch. It was 6:05. I was fifty-five minutes early. I walked into the building, located the room where the testing would take place, and then walked back outside and sat on a wooden bench in the shade. I watched a mother with two young children, about eight or nine, enter the building. I could hear shouts from kids playing somewhere inside.

The funny thing was that it should have been clear all along that prayer was useless. I remembered a General Conference when one of the apostles had said we should "pray as if everything depended on God, and work as if everything depended on us." Of *course* everything depended on us. Even they knew it.

The problem was that if I was praying as if the solution to a given problem depended on God, then psychologically, I was going to be affected by the belief he was going to help, and I was unconsciously going to work with just a little less dedication myself.

A chunky black woman in her twenties across the street was yelling at someone down the block, quite angry about some terrible thing the other person had apparently done. Curse words flew about left and right. A child walking up to the community center seemed oblivious.

It took me a minute to realize there was no one at the other end of the block.

I still allowed myself to say one complete prayer a day. As I was falling asleep next to Jeremy each evening, I thanked Heavenly Father—or the universe, or whatever—for at least ten specific good things that had happened to me that day. It was more an exercise in gratitude than a real prayer, but I still addressed it formally.

And always felt guilty immediately afterward for doing so.

Was I ever going to grow up? I was fifty-six years old, for crying out loud. I felt guilty for praying and I felt guilty for not praying. When was I ever going to just live my life?

At 6:30, I walked back into the community center and, as I'd expected, the proctors let the candidates into the multi-purpose room early to find our seats. I'd taken this test last year, done well, and then flubbed the interview. But just before the last test, I'd chatted with a few other nervous candidates, encouraging them. I didn't want to be mean today, but I had to perform better than everyone else. I couldn't afford to be "nice."

So were atheists by definition more selfish than believers?

I'd attended a meeting last night to fight for rent control, and I didn't even pay rent.

I stared at my calculator and pencils and eraser. I stared at the wall. I didn't make eye contact with any other candidates.

At 7:00, the proctors handed out the tests, and we turned them over and began working. I had to add and subtract these columns of simple figures. Multiply three dance classes times the fee. Decide if several rows of addresses were the same or different.

A child could do this.

I remembered that my boss at Rite-Aid had fired three new employees over the past few months because they couldn't count the till at the end of their shift.

There were thirty candidates in today's session taking the test, and this was only one of two sessions. I had to beat *sixty* people to get this one miserable job. Jeremy and I were going to lose the house if I didn't. I'd applied for over five hundred jobs—five hundred!—in the past year. It always came down to the interview, the six times I managed to get one. I had to do better in my interviews.

"Dear Heavenly Father—"

The realization that there was no God struck me again as if for the first time, and my throat constricted. I wasn't strong enough to do this on my own. I *needed* God.

The last question indicated that I was supposed to leave a till filled with one hundred dollars in bills. The till currently had one twenty, three fives, and a ten dollar roll of quarters. What additional amount in bills did I need to leave? I smiled. Most people were going to say they needed fifty-five dollars more, but the quarters didn't count. They weren't bills.

I finished the test, sure I'd answered every question accurately. I stood and handed my test to a proctor, the first person in the room to do so. I walked back outside, crossed the street to wait for the 48 going back to Mount Baker.

A frail, elderly black woman with osteoporosis waited patiently with her cart of groceries. A young white man talked loudly on his cell phone. An obese black woman who'd tested with me crossed the street and joined us a moment later. She looked at me and smiled.

I wanted to pray.

When the bus pulled up a few minutes later, I climbed on board, paid my fare, and found a seat on the shady side of the bus near the back door. A teenage black girl with huge earrings texted on her phone in the row in front of me. A forty-something black man in stained work clothes took a sip from an old plastic Coke bottle filled with water.

Then I stared out the window at some graffiti sprayed on a tottering wooden fence as we slowly pulled away from the curb.

The Price of Beauty

I watched as a Latina woman about forty finished eating a candy bar. It looked like a Snickers, one of my favorites, but I was trying to cut down on calories. Even if I was never going to marry, I needed to look good to set an example. People were only going to be interested in Mormonism if Mormons were people they admired.

Still chewing, the Latina peered down the street and threw the empty wrapper on the ground next to the bus stop. A Black woman in her sixties who was also waiting for the 106 motioned toward the woman and said, "Do you mind throwing your trash in the trash can?" I appreciated that she was able to say it without sounding petulant.

The Latina picked up the wrapper without complaint and carried it a few feet to a bin, pulling open the lid and tossing it in. The Black woman looked at me in disgust and rolled her eyes. The bin was a collection box for donated clothing, not a garbage can. The garbage can was two feet farther away.

The bus pulled up a few minutes later, and I climbed on behind the two women, sitting on the left side of the bus to avoid the sunlight streaming in on the right. It was mid-spring and I already found the sunshine overwhelming. Seattle could go months without rain in the summer, and it cost too much to keep my yard watered and pretty. Fortunately, we probably still had some occasional rain in the coming weeks before the driest part of the year started. But days like this worried me.

And with CO2 levels rising continually, temperatures were only going to rise. Last summer, I'd seen several well-established plants in the yards on my block die. I'd lost a young cedar I'd planted just three years ago. Forests full of beautiful trees all across the western U.S. would soon go up in flames.

The price of living in the Last Days.

On MLK, the bus picked up several Asian women dragging tiny carts filled with produce and a couple of African immigrant women wearing colorful head coverings. Even if the Asian women boarded at different stops, they all seemed to know each other. The African women seemed to recognize one another as well.

I didn't see anyone I knew.

Even people at church didn't much talk to me. The men felt uncomfortable and the women weren't interested. I considered getting a comfort dog and bringing it to church, but people thought I was odd enough already. And it wouldn't be fair for me to leave the dog home alone all day while I was at work.

My parents had died in a plane crash on their way to Hawaii seven years ago, shortly after my thirtieth birthday. I never understood why Heavenly Father hadn't taken them *after* their trip rather than before. But I supposed they were in Paradise now and would come forth in the First Resurrection.

I transferred to the 8 at the Mt. Baker Transit Center and looked out my window at the richly renovated homes in the Central District. Some were majestic and freshly painted, but they stood next to a good many decaying houses and a few that were completely boarded up. It was still prettier than my neighborhood. Even when they were new, most of the houses there hadn't been very impressive.

Except mine. I'd bought one of the most attractive ones in the area with the money my parents left me. I had two bedrooms, but one I used as a private museum. I loved amethyst in opened geodes, and fluorite, and quartz, and malachite.

When the 8 reached Madison Valley, I stepped out of the bus in front of the Bailey-Boushay house, a care facility for people living with HIV and AIDS.

There, but for the grace of God...

A block down was City People's, a nursery offering more specialized and higher priced plants than those found at Lowe's or Home Depot. I'd found a particularly attractive periwinkle here when I first moved into my house. It had now taken over the entire side yard, making even my recycle bin look pretty. These few blocks were the best part of my daily commute, walking past the high-end boutiques and restaurants and coffeeshops. Rich people always had pretty scones and scarves—and shrubs—to look at.

The Church hadn't wanted my coin collection, or my stamps, either. When I asked Bishop Moore if I could donate them, he'd turned me down. "It's too much trouble for the Church to sell this stuff. It's better if your donations are just monetary."

I'd been a little shocked. I hadn't wanted the Church to sell my collections, which I'd started while still in Primary. I'd wanted the Church to preserve them, put them in their mountain vault along with their other cherished items like the sword of Laban and the first copy of the Book of Mormon.

Everyone knew the Church kept all its important records in their secure underground fortress constructed to withstand a nuclear bomb. I didn't know why they didn't also want to keep uncirculated Buffalo nickels and Mercury dimes, unused stamps from 1934 featuring colorful engravings of the National Parks. Maybe some Art Deco lamps and vases, perhaps some gilded Victorian books with their exquisite covers. Maybe even some antique furniture, or well-crafted modern furniture, for that matter. The world would need some beauty after the devastation of the Second Coming.

If I could keep the Law of Chastity until then, I might survive Armageddon and get to enjoy the peace and happiness of the Millennium. Maybe help with reforestation. Rescue artwork that had somehow survived the Apocalypse.

When I reached the entrance to the Arboretum, I turned left to walk past the tennis court. Then a parking lot with posted signs warning people not to leave valuables in their cars. And finally I reached the entrance of the Japanese Garden.

"Morning, Wesley," said a man about my age, probably not quite forty, the head gardener. He was rolling a fertilizer spreader across the grass.

"Hi, Doug." He was a beautiful man, tall and fit, with attractive ears and shoulders just the right width. It probably wasn't emotionally healthy that these days I got turned on by the smell of manure and the sight of underarm sweat circles on a man's shirt. It looked like he winked at me, but I couldn't be sure.

I was never going to get married in the temple.

Or anywhere.

The gate to the bathrooms had already been unlocked, so I went straight to the park entrance, unlocking the heavy gate there. I set up the signs for the day, closed the second gate behind me, and used my badge to unlock the office door. It was just 9:30, and I wasn't due in for another fifteen minutes, but I always walked the entire Garden first, to see if anything new was blooming since the day before. Visitors were going to ask.

I also liked to take my time and make sure everything was in place or working properly before opening at 10:00. I set the booklets and greeting cards on the outside ledge of the ticket booth, pulled up the Point of Sale program, printed a test receipt, and read my emails.

Everyone at the park was being required to take a sensitivity training course on sexual orientation and gender identity sometime in the next two weeks. Tawona, one of the gardeners, felt a staff member had treated her unprofessionally because she was a lesbian.

Was it me, I wondered? I knew that acting on gay feelings was a sin, but I really felt that only applied to Mormons. Non-members didn't have the fullness of the gospel, so they weren't held to the same standards. I didn't consciously judge them. I envied them.

Doug probably thought he was happy. He didn't know any better.

I opened the gate again at 10:00 and started selling admission tickets. The line was always ten or fifteen people deep at the start of the day, and I always felt flustered trying to catch up. People might wait patiently for the ticket booth to open, but once it was, they acted like they were trying to get a spot in the front row at a concert.

"Two seniors and a regular adult," said an old man in front of me, hurrying as if afraid he'd have a heart attack in the next few minutes and miss seeing our waterfall. Such a thing did happen on occasion.

"Is the adult a resident of Seattle?" I asked. Seattle residents got a two dollar discount.

"No. Is there reciprocity if he has an annual pass for the Portland Japanese Garden?"

I nodded and processed the payment. Once he had the receipt in his hand, he and his group moved into the park at a leisurely pace.

Next came a woman with a stroller. Then a young British couple with student ID's. An Asian woman who was miffed her Bellevue address didn't count as Seattle. A Muslim couple with cameras. And a middle-aged white woman who tried to smuggle a small terrier in her purse. "I'm afraid no pets are allowed," I told her.

"Can I leave her with you?"

"I'm afraid not."

By 10:30, I was only greeting a new visitor every four or five minutes, a soothing pace that let me start to feel the tranquility of the park. Unfortunately, from the ticket booth, I only had one small window overlooking the Garden. My view consisted of half of a red-leafed maple tree and the top of an azalea with purple flowers. Pretty, but sometimes I still felt like a prisoner looking through the bars of my cell window.

So close to beauty but surrounded by walls covered with work schedules, procedures, and shelves of receipt paper and money logs. If things were quiet, I might open the door and get a glimpse of the path leading to the tea house or, on a good day, Doug working in the rhododendron glen. The gardeners tried to do their most intrusive work before visitors were allowed in, of course.

We opened at noon on Mondays to give the gardeners more freedom at least one day of the week. If I was scheduled to work that day, I always came an hour early. I pretended to stroll slowly through the Garden to enjoy the scenery, and I truly did enjoy it, but part of the scenery was the back of Doug's head.

If he didn't know I was looking at him, he wouldn't be tempted to look back. Not that I was likely to be very tempting. I was only ten pounds overweight, but almost all of it seemed to be in my face. Real chipmunks were cute, but thirty-seven-year-old men with chubby faces weren't.

I'd wanted to donate the two books I owned featuring male nudes to the Church, too, but I wasn't stupid enough to offer. The men were photographed alone, not doing anything sexual, just standing or sitting while looking beautiful. Surely, during the Millennium, with Satan locked up and no longer able to tempt anyone, people would be free to appreciate the beauty of the human form.

I wanted to donate my fossil collection to the Church, too, and my handmade quilts. I designed patchwork portraits of my favorite temples using graph paper. Only a handful of the hundred or so temples worldwide were very pretty. So many were cookie cutter. Such great expense for lackluster façades. It almost seemed a sin. But I did manage to piece together spectacular quilt tops of a good fifteen of the best temples.

The bishop didn't want those, either.

But I was never going to be able to have any kids. What other kind of legacy could I leave behind?

Maybe I could work in a Church museum during the Millennium, if members could donate paintings and sculptures and jewelry now. Everything could be taken out of the vault as the good people who were allowed to live rose up out of the rubble and rebuilt.

I remembered that even as a cashier, I was considered essential personnel for the City because in the event of an earthquake or tsunami or other disaster, I'd be called up as a Parks employee to help operate shelters set up on public grounds for displaced survivors. A full ten percent of the land within city limits was dedicated to parks.

Maybe it would be okay under such dire circumstances for Doug and me to sleep in the same tent.

Perhaps we'd even have to share a blanket.

The phone rang. I spent the next couple of minutes selling tickets to one of the tea ceremonies held in the tea house, a tedious process made worse when I had to tell the customer that the tea ceremony tickets only granted them access to the ceremony, but in order to get there, they'd also need access to the park, requiring an additional admission fee. I transferred the call to a secure line so I could get the customer's credit card information and told them we'd have their tickets waiting for them the day of the ceremony.

A white woman with a ten-year-old girl had come up to the window while I was on the phone and now seemed relieved to finally be able to speak. "Can we feed the koi yet?"

"Not until May 12." It was a week and a half away.

"Aw," said the little girl.

"The water's still too cold," I explained. "The koi's digestive system goes into a kind of hibernation until the water warms up to a certain temperature."

"Aw," the little girl repeated.

"But the pink azaleas along the north end of the pond will be in full bloom by then. And the wisteria a week after that. It'll be a great time to come back." Flowers were not really the focus of Japanese gardens, but it was what so many visitors wanted to see.

The girl seemed to consider this information and nodded reluctantly. I sold the mother two tickets and then waited on the next visitor in line, a woman from Poland. She was followed by two young men from Germany carrying backpacks. A huge percentage of our guests were tourists. I enjoyed surprising the ones from France with the French I'd learned on my mission.

Such a beautiful language. And Paris was the most beautiful city I'd ever seen. I sure hoped it would survive the End of Days the way it had World War II.

I couldn't help but think how great it would be to walk along the Seine with Doug. What would it be like to hold his hand? We didn't need to have a sexual relationship. I just wanted to be close to him. We could be friends. Kissing him on the forehead wasn't breaking any covenants, was it?

I wondered if Doug could get a job working at the Luxembourg Gardens. Or the Tuileries. Or any of the other beautiful gardens in Paris. Living with him there would undoubtedly be wonderful. Even seeing him a few fleeting moments in this idyllic spot in central Seattle was lovely.

A young straight couple in their mid-twenties, holding hands and looking all googly eyed at each other, came up to buy tickets. "When you take your pictures," I told them, "just stay on the path." They nodded and moved into the park, their shoulders touching.

Every day when I got home from work, the first thing I did was pull up YouTube and listen to Meghan Trainor and John Legend singing, "I'm Gonna Love You Like I'm Gonna Lose You."

What if Doug and I didn't both make it to the Millennium? I didn't know if I could endure a thousand years without seeing him. If I could bring him into the gospel, though, he could be a better person. But once he knew the truth, he'd be responsible for living all the rules. He might have a better chance if I didn't say anything at all.

An old woman tapped on my window.

"Yes?"

"There's a funny smell in the Garden today."

I smiled, thinking of the fresh fertilizer. "I'll let the gardeners know," I said. It's what people wanted to hear.

A little later, an elderly man with a cane tapped on my window. "There's a branch on one of the cherry trees that's not blossoming very well."

"I'll let the gardeners know straight away." In two weeks, the man wouldn't be able to remember which branch had offended him so strongly. But if he came back, he'd probably find fault with something else. Some people seemed perpetually unable to be happy even in this beautiful spot.

My parents had been unhappy I wasn't married yet. I wished I'd found a way to tell them why. Were they looking down on me from the Spirit World now rooting for me? If only they could whisper in Doug's ear to go to a movie with me sometime. But perhaps that was the last thing they wanted.

My Home Teachers had rarely come by even when that program had been pushed every week. Now that it had been discontinued, no one from church ever came by at all.

Around 1:00, just after one of the volunteers started her free guided tour, a plump woman about my age ran up to the window. "An eagle just grabbed one of the koi and flew off!"

I nodded. Such an attack was rare and only occurred if there weren't too many visitors that day. Raccoons ate some of the fish, too, when they came into the park at night. I wanted to say, "How fortunate to witness something so incredible," but I knew that wasn't what she wanted to hear.

"Well, do something!"

"I'll let the gardeners know."

People also expected us to stop traffic down the main road through the Arboretum, which passed just to the east of the Garden. "It's too loud. It's not like a real Japanese Garden here at all. It's not authentic." One of the most famous gardens in

Japan was located right next to a hospital, with sirens blasting through the air every few minutes.

"I'll let my supervisor know."

As if temporal authorities could fix everything. Even Church headquarters couldn't solve impossible problems. I remembered when I worked as the ward financial secretary a couple of years ago. Apparently, the bishop had felt inspired to call me because I could operate a cash drawer.

I only held the position for fifteen months, but I remembered the time the bank found a counterfeit hundred dollar bill in our deposit. Three different families had paid their tithing with cash that week, so there was no way to know who had accidentally given us the bill. But Salt Lake sent out an auditor to track down the culprit.

The cost of the plane ticket alone was more than a hundred dollars. But the auditor insisted that the family who handed us the bad bill make good on the payment. He spent three days going through records, but even as a lowly cashier, it seemed clear to me his goal was unattainable. He eventually flew back to Salt Lake without having generated any replacement funds.

How much was balancing to the penny worth?

Or was this all really about the price of honesty?

It was shortly after this incident that I finally told the bishop the reason I wasn't married was because I was gay. Two weeks later, I was released from my calling. I'd have felt hurt if it hadn't been such a relief to no longer have to devote ten hours a week tracking how much more money other members of the congregation made than I did.

I needed a better job. Even with my inheritance, I needed to work more than thirty hours a week. But walking through the Garden every workday was worth something, too.

Seeing Doug was worth something.

The phone rang again. But it wasn't a customer on the phone this time. It was my supervisor, Greta. Her office was off site, so there were plenty of shifts when I never saw her. "Everything good today, Wesley?"

"We're getting low on maps of the Garden," I said, "and a couple of the greeting cards. I'll send you an email."

"Thank you. Got enough ones for the rest of your shift?"

I was working two shifts today, from 10:00 to closing time at 7:00. Pamela had to do something with her daughter this afternoon and asked me to cover for her. I was usually the one to fill in when the other cashiers had a medical appointment or went on vacation. It didn't really bother me. What else did I have to do? "Everything's good so far."

"Great. I'll see you tomorrow."

I sold admission tickets to a white man and his Asian wife. Then there was a group of four Indians. Followed by two Asian students from Seattle Central College. A white woman who looked dressed for a high-powered business meeting. And a Finnish girl with bright pink hair.

I'd checked the movie *Tom of Finland* out of the library a few weeks ago. I knew I wasn't supposed to watch gay movies, but it was about art, and I couldn't resist. I would never buy one of his books, of course. And yet the thought that his sexualized drawings might not survive an approaching worldwide conflagration brought me no joy.

"Ma'am," I said to the next woman who came to my window, "I'm afraid no food or drink is allowed in the park." She was already aware of the rule, of course. I'd seen her hiding a sandwich in her purse before walking up to the window. I was always surprised by how many people coming here specifically for an experience in a pristine setting left garbage on the walkways.

"I'll keep my trash in my purse," she said.

I shook my head. "You can eat out in the courtyard and go into the park afterwards."

She curled her lip. "I don't know why you don't just put garbage cans on the paths."

"There's a bench right over there." I pointed toward the water fountain. I remembered her now as the visitor who'd dropped her sunglasses in the pond a couple of weeks ago and demanded the gardeners come running to fish them out of the muck.

"I have an annual pass," the woman said.

"Oh, excellent!" I said. "Thank you for your support! I'll record your card number after you've finished eating."

The woman looked like she might say something else, but she finally walked back out of the gate. Visitors often asked why we didn't sell hot tea. Or sushi. One guy about a year ago even tried to order tempura.

I saw that the woman had gone back to her car, and I didn't see anyone else approaching, so I put a "Back in 5 minutes" sign on the window and hurried to the bathroom behind the ticket booth.

Sometimes, at the end of my shift, I would beat off while thinking of Doug. I felt closer to him if I did it here rather than at home. I knew masturbation might keep me out of the Millennium, but all I could think about was the fact that since Doug didn't know any better, it might not keep *him* out. So I fantasized about him fantasizing about me.

There was no time for that now, though. I urinated, washed my hands, and hurried back to the ticket booth.

The rest of the afternoon passed routinely. One visitor tried to smuggle out a turtle, but thankfully, I was able to spot it in time. Another guy grumbled that "a mean gardener" ordered him to stop walking on the moss. Sometimes, Tawona worked late into the afternoon, but I made myself believe it was Doug lingering about hoping to get another glimpse of me before the end of the day.

An old man tripped on some stone steps at the far end of the garden but seemed okay. I still had him fill out an incident report. And someone called on the phone asking if they could hold their wedding in the park.

"Not at this garden," I said, "but you can have your wedding in Kubota Garden in south Seattle." It was another lovely park, a few blocks from my home in Rainier Beach, but it was not as heavily manicured and had no admission fee.

The house I'd bought six years ago was a 1910 Craftsman cottage formerly owned by a gardener who ran a nursery that was in competition with Kubota back in the day.

It was clear no gardener lived there now.

I wondered if Doug would be happy puttering around the yard if he moved in with me. We could sleep under the quilt I'd pieced together of the Logan temple.

I'd almost pay the price of exaltation to be with Doug a few, brief, fleeting moments. Flowers were still pretty, even if they only bloomed for a week.

"Can I fly my drone camera over the park?" asked a tall, white man with braids.

"I'm afraid not." Of course, if he hadn't been nice enough to ask, how would I have been able to stop him? "We do have a photography pass," I said, "that gives you access to the Garden at times it's not open to the public. We even let you use tripods, which we don't let regular visitors do."

He was a tourist, though, and passed on the offer.

The number of visitors dropped to a trickle the last couple of hours. Someone bought a koi flag, and a young woman debated for almost ten minutes on which T-shirt she wanted to buy. We only offered two styles. Another visitor complained about the smell, which must surely have dissipated a great deal by this point.

Was Doug still out there this late in the day, spreading extra fertilizer to be near me?

It was like being on the other side of the veil, close enough to touch but still not able to see him.

I'd taken a picture of Doug with my phone once and then printed it out and put it on my bedstand. He was the last thing I saw before going to sleep every night and the first thing I saw when I woke up.

Inviting him to dinner wouldn't be breaking the Law of Chastity, would it?

About ten minutes to 7:00, I pulled the front gate almost closed and did my walk around the park, shooing the last guests out. It was clear the gardeners had all long since left. I fantasized sometimes about finding Doug sitting on a bench waiting for me, but it hadn't happened yet.

On my closing loop, I carried a large plastic cup so I could gather the change people left at three of our concrete lanterns. God only knew how the tradition got started. It certainly wasn't part of the history of such gardens. We deposited the coins as a donation once a week. Someone left a wheat penny today.

There was no real way to guarantee everyone was gone from the park. Too many hiding spots. But at 7:00, I closed the gate and then counted my money, sealed my deposit bag, completed the last of my closing paperwork, and then set the alarm.

I looked out over the Garden one last time for the day, locked the entrance gate, and then locked the gate in front of the bathrooms. I walked back to Madison Street and past the boutiques and coffeehouses and restaurants until I reached the stop for the 8.

I sat on the left side of the bus to avoid as much of the direct sunlight as I could. While waiting for the 106 on Rainier, I saw a chunky Black woman about my age wearing a tight mini dress. The way she was sitting on the bench made her skirt hike up, revealing to anyone interested that she wasn't wearing underwear.

I turned away and counted sixteen gobs of spit on the sidewalk where other people had been waiting.

When the bus came a few minutes later, I hopped on and headed home, where I had a nice TV dinner waiting for me in the freezer. A Lean Cuisine, so I could set a good example for Doug.

Books by Johnny Townsend

Thanks for reading! If you enjoyed this book, could you please take a few minutes to write a review online? Reviews are helpful both to me as an author and to other readers, so we'd all sincerely appreciate your writing one! And if you did enjoy the book, here are some others I've written you might want to look up:

Mormon Underwear

A Gay Mormon Missionary in Pompeii

The Golem of Rabbi Loew

Marginal Mormons

Gay Gaslighting

Mormon Misfits

Going-Out-Of-Religion Sale

Escape from Zion

Gayrabian Nights

Invasion of the Spirit Snatchers

Sins of the Saints

Out of the Missionary's Closet

Sexual Solidarity

The Mysterious Madness of Mormons

Human Compassion for Beginners

Breaking the Promise of the Promised Land

I Will, Through the Veil

Am I My Planet's Keeper?

Have Your Cum and Eat It, Too

Strangers with Benefits

Constructing Equity

Wake Up and Smell the Missionaries

Racism by Proxy

Orgy at the STD Clinic

Please Evacuate

Recommended Daily Humanity

The Camper Killings

An Eternity of Mirrors: Best Short Stories of Johnny Townsend

Kinky Quilts: Patchwork Designs for Gay Men

Inferno in the French Quarter: The UpStairs Lounge Fire

Latter-Gay Saints: An Anthology of Gay Mormon Fiction (co-editor)

Available from your favorite online or neighborhood bookstore.

Wondering what some of those other books are about? Read on!

Invasion of the Spirit Snatchers

During the Apocalypse, a group of Mormon survivors in Hurricane, Utah gather in the home of the Relief Society president, telling stories to pass the time as they ration their food storage and await the Second Coming. But this is no ordinary group of Mormons—or perhaps it is. They are the faithful, feminist, gay, apostate, and repentant, all working together to help each other through the darkest days any of them have yet seen.

Gayrabian Nights

Gayrabian Nights is a twist on the well-known classic, *1001 Arabian Nights*, in which Scheherazade, under the threat of death if she ceases to captivate King Shahryar's attention, enchants him through a series of mysterious, adventurous, and romantic tales.

In this variation, a male escort, invited to the hotel room of a closeted, homophobic Mormon senator, learns that the man is poised to vote on a piece of anti-gay legislation the following morning. To prevent him from sleeping, so that the exhausted senator will miss casting his vote on the Senate floor, the escort entertains him with stories of homophobia, celibacy, mixed orientation marriages, reparative therapy, coming out, first love, gay marriage, and long-term successful gay relationships. The escort crafts the stories to give the senator a crash course in gay culture and sensibilities, hoping to bring the man closer to accepting his own sexual orientation.

Inferno in the French Quarter: The UpStairs Lounge Fire

On Gay Pride Day in 1973, someone set the entrance to a French Quarter gay bar on fire. In the terrible inferno that followed, thirty-two people lost their lives, including a third of the local congregation of the Metropolitan Community Church, their pastor burning to death halfway out a second-story window as he tried to claw his way to freedom. A mother who'd gone to the bar with her two gay sons died alongside them. A man who'd helped his friend escape first was found dead near the fire escape. Two children waited outside a movie theater across town for a father and step-father who would never pick them up. During this era of rampant homophobia, several families refused to claim the bodies, and many churches refused to bury the dead. Author Johnny Townsend pored through old records and tracked down survivors of the fire as well as relatives and friends of those killed to compile this fascinating account of a forgotten moment in gay history.

A Gay Mormon Missionary in Pompeii

What is a gay Mormon missionary doing in Italy? He is trying to save his own soul as well as the souls of others. In these tales chronicling the two-year mission of Robert Anderson, we see a young man tormented by his inability to be the man the Church says he should be. In addition to his personal hell, Anderson faces a major earthquake, organized crime, a serious bus accident, and much more. He copes with horrendous mission leaders and his own suicidal tendencies. But one day, he meets another missionary who loves him, and his world changes forever.

The Golem of Rabbi Loew

Jacob and Esau Cohen are the closest of brothers. In fact, they're lovers. A doctor tries to combine canine genes with those of Jews, to improve their chances of surviving a hostile world. A Talmudic scholar dates an escort. A scientist tries to develop the "God spot" in the brains of his patients in hopes of creating a messiah.

A Jew-by-Choice navigates Jewish/Muslim relations during Pesach. A gay Lubavitcher dating a Catholic is attacked and left for dead but becomes a police officer in response. The Golem of Prague is really Rabbi Loew's secret lover.

While some of the Jews in Townsend's book are Orthodox, this collection of Jewish stories most certainly is not.

Am I My Planet's Keeper?

Global Warming. Climate Change. Climate Crisis. Climate Emergency. Whatever label we use, we are facing one of the greatest challenges to the survival of life as we know it.

But while addressing greenhouse gases is perhaps our most urgent need, it's not our only task. We must also address toxic waste, pollution, habitat destruction, and our other contributions to the world's sixth mass extinction event.

In order to do that, we must simultaneously address the unmet human needs that keep us distracted from deeper engagement in stabilizing our climate: moderating economic inequality, guaranteeing healthcare to all, and ensuring education for everyone.

And to accomplish *that*, we must unite to combat the monied forces that use fear, prejudice, and misinformation to manipulate us.

It's a daunting task. But success is our only option.

Wake Up and Smell the Missionaries

Two Mormon missionaries in Italy discover they share the same rare ability—both can emit pheromones on demand. At first, they playfully compete in the hills of Frascati to see who can tempt "investigators" most. But soon they're targeting each other non-stop.

Can two immature young men learn to control their "superpower" to live a normal life…and develop genuine love? Even as their relationship is threatened by the attentions of another man?

They seem just on the verge of success when a massive earthquake leaves them trapped under the rubble of their apartment in Castellammare.

With night falling and temperatures dropping, can they dig themselves out in time to save themselves? And will their injuries destroy the ability that brought them together in the first place?

Orgy at the STD Clinic

Todd Tillotson is struggling to move on after his husband is killed in a hit and run attack a year earlier during a Black Lives Matter protest in Seattle.

In this novel set entirely on public transportation, we watch as Todd, isolated throughout the pandemic, battles desperation in his attempt to safely reconnect with the world.

Will he find love again, even casual friendship, or will he simply end up another crazy old man on the bus?

Things don't look good until a man whose face he can't even see sits down beside him despite the raging variants.

And asks him a question that will change his life.

Please Evacuate

A gay, partygoing New Yorker unconcerned about the future or the unsustainability of capitalism is hit by a truck and thrust into a straight man's body half a continent away. As Hunter tries to figure out what's happening, he's caught up in another disaster, a wildfire sweeping through a Colorado community, the flames overtaking him and several schoolchildren as they flee.

When he awakens, Hunter finds himself in the body of yet another man, this time in northern Italy, a former missionary about to marry a young Mormon woman. Still piecing together this new reality, and beginning to embrace his latest identity, Hunter fights for his life in a devastating flash flood along with his wife *and* his new husband.

He's an aging worker in drought-stricken Texas, a nurse at an assisted living facility in the direct path of a hurricane, an advocate for the unhoused during a freak Seattle blizzard.

We watch as Hunter is plunged into life after life, finally recognizing the futility of only looking out for #1 and understanding the part he must play in addressing the global climate crisis…if he ever gets another chance.

Recommended Daily Humanity

A checklist of human rights must include basic housing, universal healthcare, equitable funding for public schools, and tuition-free college and vocational training.

In addition to the basics, though, we need much more to fully thrive. Subsidized childcare, universal pre-K, a universal basic income, subsidized high-speed internet, net neutrality, fare-free public transit (plus *more* public transit), and medically assisted death for the terminally ill who want it.

None of this will matter, though, if we neglect to address the rapidly worsening climate crisis.

Sound expensive? It is.

But not as expensive as refusing to implement these changes. The cost of climate disasters each year has grown to staggering figures. And the cost of social and political upheaval from not meeting the needs of suffering workers, families, and individuals may surpass even that.

It's best we understand that the vast sums required to enact meaningful change are an investment which will pay off not only in some indeterminate future but in fact almost immediately. And without these adjustments to our lifestyles and values, there may very well not be a future capable of sustaining freedom and democracy…or even civilization itself.

The Camper Killings

When a homeless man is found murdered a few blocks from Morgan Beylerian's house in south Seattle, everyone seems to consider the body just so much additional trash to be cleared from the neighborhood. But Morgan liked the guy. They used to chat when Morgan brought Nick groceries once a week.

And the brutal way the man was killed reminds Morgan of their shared Mormon heritage, back when the faithful agreed to have their throats slit if they ever revealed temple secrets.

Did Nick's former wife take action when her ex-husband refused to grant a temple divorce? Did his murder have something to do with the public accusations that brought an end to his promising career?

Morgan does his best to investigate when no one else seems to care, but it isn't easy as a man living paycheck to paycheck himself, only able to pursue his investigation via public transit.

As he continues his search for the killer, Morgan's friends withdraw and his husband threatens to leave. When another homeless man is killed and Morgan is accused of the crime, things look even bleaker.

But his troubles aren't over yet.

Will Morgan find the killer before the killer finds him?

Sins of the Saints

In this collection of stories by ex-Mormon author Johnny Townsend, we see a missionary cope with the startling discovery that his companion has been translated off the face of the Earth. A teenage girl pretends to be her brother so she can "hold the priesthood" for at least a day.

A young man taught that loved ones watch over family members from the Other Side keeps imagining his grandmother catching him masturbating. A former prostitute, now a faithful Latter-day Saint, finds that some of her fellow congregants can't get beyond her past. A schizophrenic Single Adult leads a secret life no one in her congregation suspects.

Escape from Zion

In these short stories by ex-Mormon author Johnny Townsend, parents hire men to pose as the Three Nephites to teach their children the Book of Mormon is true. A shy single woman meets the man of her dreams at an endoscopy party.

An anti-Mormon mob threatens a church outing. A deceased sinner plots to break out of Spirit Prison. Aliens visiting the UN reveal that God really does live on the planet Kolob. Mormons survive the zombie apocalypse because of their two-year supply of food. A young couple desperately try to escape after America becomes a theocracy.

Another fun collection from the author of *Recommended Daily Humanity* and *Please Evacuate*.

The Mysterious Madness of Mormons

When religious indoctrination clashes with reality, the outcome can't always be predicted. In these stories by the author of *Please Evacuate* and *Inferno in the French Quarter*, a Seminary teacher threatens to kill his students. A schizophrenic woman in a hurricane evacuation shelter finds love. A Relief Society president's silicone breast implants develop into a new life form. A sister missionary suffocating under family pressure volunteers to be held hostage during a bank robbery. A teenage girl is haunted by the ghost of Emma Smith. A devout Mormon takes up sex work to raise money to help the poor.

Sometimes, behavior that seems perfectly reasonable in one culture can seem disturbing to those outside it. But whether reasonable or disturbing, their stories can also make compelling reading.

What Readers Have Said

Townsend's stories are "a gay *Portnoy's Complaint* of Mormonism. Salacious, sweet, sad, insightful, insulting, religiously ethnic, quirky-faithful, and funny."

D. Michael Quinn, author of *The Mormon Hierarchy: Origins of Power*

"Told from a believably conversational first-person perspective, [*A Gay Mormon Missionary in Pompeii*'s] novelistic focus on Anderson's journey to thoughtful self-acceptance allows for greater character development than often seen in short stories, which makes this well-paced work rich and satisfying, and one of Townsend's strongest. An extremely important contribution to the field of Mormon fiction." Named to Kirkus Reviews' Best of 2011.

Kirkus Reviews

"The thirteen stories in *Mormon Underwear* capture this struggle [between Mormonism and homosexuality] with humor, sadness, insight, and sometimes shocking details....*Mormon Underwear* provides compelling stories, literally from the inside-out."

Niki D'Andrea, *Phoenix New Times*

"Townsend's lively writing style and engaging characters [in *Zombies for Jesus*] make for stories which force us to wake up, smell the (prohibited) coffee, and review our attitudes with regard to reading dogma so doggedly. These are tales which revel in the individual tics and quirks which make us human, Mormon or not, gay or not…"

A.J. Kirby, *The Short Review*

"The Rift," from *A Gay Mormon Missionary in Pompeii*, is a "fascinating tale of an untenable situation…a *tour de force*."

David Lenson, editor, *The Massachusetts Review*

"Pronouncing the Apostrophe," from *The Golem of Rabbi Loew*, is "quiet and revealing, an intriguing tale…"

Sima Rabinowitz, Literary Magazine Review, *NewPages.com*

The Circumcision of God is "a collection of short stories that consider the imperfect, silenced majority of Mormons, who may in fact be [the Church's] best hope….[The book leaves] readers regretting the church's willingness to marginalize those who best exemplify its ideals: those who love fiercely despite all obstacles, who brave challenges at great personal risk and who always choose the hard, higher road."

Kirkus Reviews

In *Mormon Fairy Tales*, Johnny Townsend displays "both a wicked sense of irony and a deep well of compassion."

Kel Munger, *Sacramento News and Review*

Zombies for Jesus is "eerie, erotic, and magical."

Publishers Weekly

"While [Townsend's] many touching vignettes draw deeply from Mormon mythology, history, spirituality and culture, [*Mormon Fairy Tales*] is neither a gaudy act of proselytism nor angry protest literature from an ex-believer. Like all good fiction, his stories are simply about the joys, the hopes and the sorrows of people."

Kirkus Reviews

"In *Inferno in the French Quarter* author Johnny Townsend restores this tragic event [the UpStairs Lounge fire] to its proper place in LGBT history and reminds us that the victims of the blaze were not just 'statistics,' but real people with real lives, families, and friends."

Jesse Monteagudo, *The Bilerico Project*

In *Inferno in the French Quarter*, "Townsend's heart-rending descriptions of the victims…seem to [make them] come alive once more."

Kit Van Cleave, *OutSmart Magazine*

Marginal Mormons is "an irreverent, honest look at life outside the mainstream Mormon Church….Throughout his musings on sin and forgiveness, Townsend beautifully demonstrates his characters' internal, perhaps irreconcilable struggles….Rather than anger and disdain, he offers an honest portrayal of people searching for meaning and community in their lives, regardless of their life choices or secrets." Named to Kirkus Reviews' Best of 2012.

Kirkus Reviews

The stories in *The Mormon Victorian Society* "register the new openness and confidence of gay life in the age of same-sex marriage….What hasn't changed is Townsend's wry, conversational prose, his subtle evocations of character and social dynamics, and his deadpan humor. His warm empathy still glows in this intimate yet clear-eyed engagement with Mormon theology and folkways. Funny, shrewd and finely wrought dissections of the awkward contradictions—and surprising harmonies—between conscience and desire." Named to Kirkus Reviews' Best of 2013.

Kirkus Reviews

"This collection of short stories [*The Mormon Victorian Society*] featuring gay Mormon characters slammed [me] in the face from the first page, wrestled my heart and mind to the floor, and left me panting and wanting more by the end. Johnny Townsend has created so many memorable characters in such few pages. I went weeks thinking about this book. It truly touched me."

Tom Webb, *A Bear on Books*

Dragons of the Book of Mormon is an "entertaining collection….Townsend's prose is sharp, clear, and easy to read, and his characters are well rendered…"

Publishers Weekly

"The pre-eminent documenter of alternative Mormon lifestyles…Townsend has a deep understanding of his characters, and his limpid prose, dry humor and well-grounded (occasionally magical) realism make their spiritual conundrums both compelling and entertaining. [*Dragons of the Book of Mormon* is] [a]nother of Townsend's critical but affectionate and absorbing tours of Mormon discontent." Named to Kirkus Reviews' Best of 2014.

Kirkus Reviews

In *Gayrabian Nights*, "Townsend's prose is always limpid and evocative, and…he finds real drama and emotional depth in the most ordinary of lives."

Kirkus Reviews

Gayrabian Nights is a "complex revelation of how seriously soul damaging the denial of the true self can be."

Ryan Rhodes, author of *Free Electricity*

Gayrabian Nights "was easily the most original book I've read all year. Funny, touching, topical, and thoroughly enjoyable."

Rainbow Awards

Lying for the Lord is "one of the most gripping books that I've picked up for quite a while. I love the author's writing style, alternately cynical, humorous, biting, scathing, poignant, and touching…. This is the third book of his that I've read, and all are equally engaging. These are stories that need to be told, and the author does it in just the right way."

Heidi Alsop, *Ex-Mormon Foundation Board Member*

In *Lying for the Lord*, Townsend "gets under the skin of his characters to reveal their complexity and conflicts….shrewd, evocative [and] wryly humorous."

Kirkus Reviews

In *Missionaries Make the Best Companions*, "the author treats the clash between religious dogma and liberal humanism with vivid realism, sly humor, and subtle feeling as his characters try to figure out their true missions in life. Another of Townsend's rich dissections of Mormon failures and uncertainties…" Named to Kirkus Reviews' Best of 2015.

Kirkus Reviews

In *Invasion of the Spirit Snatchers*, "Townsend, a confident and practiced storyteller, skewers the hypocrisies and eccentricities of his characters with precision and affection. The outlandish framing narrative is the most consistent source of shock and humor, but the stories do much to ground the reader in the world—or former world—of the characters….A funny, charming tale about a group of Mormons facing the end of the world."

Kirkus Reviews

"Townsend's collection [*The Washing of Brains*] once again displays his limpid, naturalistic prose, skillful narrative chops, and his subtle insights into psychology…Well-crafted dispatches on the clash between religion and self-fulfillment…"

Kirkus Reviews

"While the author is generally at his best when working as a satirist, there are some fine, understated touches in these tales [*The Last Days Linger*] that will likely affect readers in subtle ways….readers should come away impressed by the deep empathy he shows for all his characters—even the homophobic ones."

Kirkus Reviews

"Written in a conversational style that often uses stories and personal anecdotes to reveal larger truths, this immensely approachable book [*Racism by Proxy*] skillfully serves its intended audience of White readers grappling with complex questions regarding race, history, and identity. The author's frequent references to the Church of Jesus Christ of Latter-day Saints may be too niche for readers unfamiliar with its idiosyncrasies, but Townsend generally strikes a perfect balance of humor, introspection, and reasoned arguments that will engage even skeptical readers."

Kirkus Reviews

Orgy at the STD Clinic portrays "an all-too real scenario that Townsend skewers to wincingly accurate proportions…[with]

instant classic moments courtesy of his punchy, sassy, sexy lead character…"

Jim Piechota, *Bay Area Reporter*

Orgy at the STD Clinic is "…a triumph of humane sensibility. A richly textured saga that brilliantly captures the fraying social fabric of contemporary life." Named to Kirkus Reviews' Best Indie Books of 2022.

Kirkus Reviews

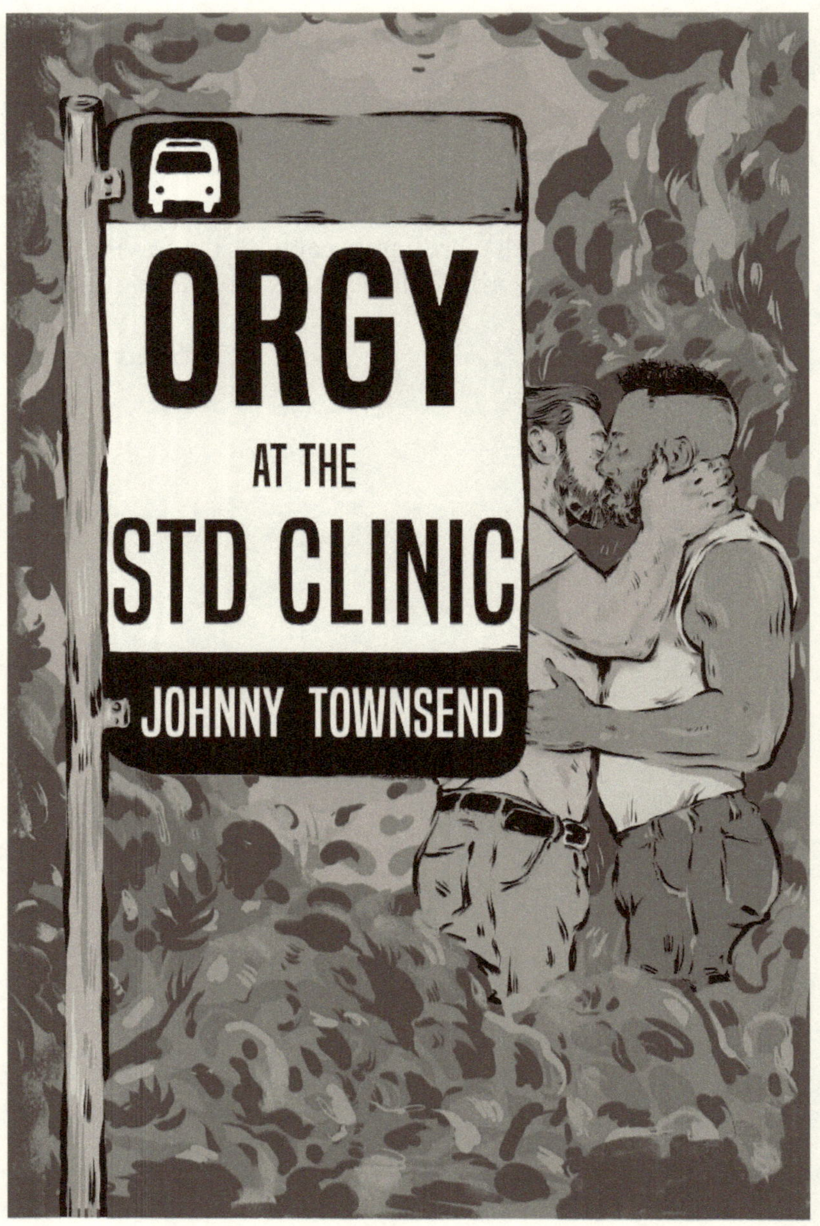

ORGY
AT THE
STD CLINIC
JOHNNY TOWNSEND

HAVE YOUR CUM AND EAT IT, TOO
JOHNNY TOWNSEND